THE EYE THIEF

THE EYE THIEF
BY
TARA McLEOD MOORE

FUN IDEAS PRODUCTIONS
2014

The Eye Thief

© 2014 Tara McLeod Moore

This book is a work of fiction. Names, characters, places and incidents either are the product of the author's imagination or are used fictitiously, except where noted. Any resemblance to actual persons, living or dead, events or locales is entirely coincidental except where indicated.

For information, address:
Fun Ideas Productions
P.O. Box 2616
Saratoga, CA 95070
http:.//funideas.50webs.com

Cover painting by Richard Becker; Model: José-Raúl Campaña
Graphic art and cover design by Jerry Cornell
Typesetting and layout by Mark Arnold

Published in the USA by Fun Ideas Productions.

Library of Congress Cataloging-in-Publication Data

McLeod Moore, Tara.
The Eye Thief / by Tara McLeod Moore.
Includes index.
ISBN 978-0-578-15482-4
          I. McLeod Moore, Tara. II. Fiction Novel. III. Title.

DEDICATION:
Dedicated to the memory of Alan McLeod Sims
(January 20, 1935 - October 6, 2012)

Mostly, this story is inspired by the generosity, caring, and storytelling ability of my father, who greatly helped a young boy in Mexico. A lot of what occurs in this story actually happened. However, events and people have been telescoped, combined, and remixed, in order to make a great story. Some ideas also came from studying about and traveling to Mexico. Other ideas came from my long experiences with teenagers: being one, raising two, and teaching many thousands of them. Finally, as my father helped this young boy, he also shared with me the harrowing experiences of the families living there. I now share them with you. I hope you enjoy this story.

SPECIAL THANKS:

To Mark Arnold, who helped me to bring this book to completion, to Eirene and Nick Butterfield for reading my book, to all of my English teachers and to the members of the Willow Glen Writer's club. Thank you to José-Raúl Campaña, who generously allowed his image from his Lincoln High School days in San Jose to be used as the model for the cover. I would also like to thank Dr. Martin Fishman for allowing me to include his real contributions, which are part of the inspirations for this story.

CONTENTS

FOREWORD

by Mark Arnold,

Author and Comic Book and Animation Historian

Tara Moore's story begins innocently, but soon makes a wrong turn: "Julian saw a clear plastic bag full of the kind of needles doctors on TV gave shots with. 'Hey, look at these!' he called. He held up the bag of hypodermic syringes. He held them up for Ricky to admire.

'¡Ay! ¡Bueno!' Ricky hooted, and grinned. 'Good squirt guns!'

Julian filled the syringes with salty water and wrapped them back into the bandana. They trudged through the sand and climbed back up the stairs.

The needles were soon emptied, and they looked for a place to refill them. There was a small lumber mill along the road, with high brick walls, where Julian and his father had worked. It had a small spigot at one corner.

Ricky turned on the spigot, and all four of them held the needles under the running water, drawing up the plunger to pull in the water. Julian's would not fill, so he backed away and crouched down over the syringe. He pulled the plunger to release it from the needle section. Something seemed to be jammed. Julian stared down at the syringe and pulled out the plunger slowly from behind. It slipped, and then stuck again. He pulled at it harder. Suddenly, the plunger came out with a pop, sending the syringe, needle first, into his eye.

Julian pulled it out, throwing down the needle. He clasped his other hand desperately over his eye and howled in pain...."

With these words, the saga of *The Eye Thief* begins. Author, Tara Moore, displays the story writing talents of any major author with a shocking and suspenseful tale that reveals one startling revelation after another. It has the added bonus of being based on truth, which makes what happens all the more frightening.

Moore deftly uses her skills as a writer to carve out a tale based on the underhanded betrayal goes on in countries like Mexico with regularity. You too will be engrossed by the adventures of Julian and Ricky, Esther and María, Marisol, Manuel, and the shady Dr. Bella in a story with bribery, extortion, blackmail, murder set in hospitals, courtrooms, and back alleys.

The action in *The Eye Thief* will surprise you and compel you and you will be unable to put it down until its conclusion...

CHAPTER 1 NEEDLES

Two fourteen-year-olds rummaged in a dumpster behind a medical clinic. The clinic's unlocked, large dumpster contained surgical scrubs, bags of used ear inspection cones, plastic tubing, half empty blood vials, and many other interesting items.

Ricky, thin and dark-skinned, but with light brown hair, found a bag of clean-looking rubber gloves for making water balloons. He blew one up and whispered to Julian, "They look like chickens when you do this." He held the inflated glove over his head and clucked like a chicken.

Julian laughed, saying, "What a skinny chicken you are!"

Julian looked older due to his height, and had dubbed Ricky a "natural short stop." Julian saw a clear plastic bag full of the kind of needles doctors on TV gave shots with. "Hey, look at these!" he called. He held up the bag of hypodermic syringes for Ricky to admire.

"*¡Ay! ¡Bueno!*" Ricky hooted, and grinned. "Good squirt guns!"

Their girlfriends stood several yards away. Esther frowning and keeping a look out. María smiled and said to her, "Relax! They will be out in a second." Then she called to the boys, "Hurry up!"

Julian said to Ricky, "Let's go!" They were about to jump out, when a man with a shaved head and round glasses, wearing a white lab smock, emerged from the clinic door.

"Oh no! Get down!" Esther ordered.

The boys ducked back into the dumpster. The girls slowly walked away from it, but the man in the lab smock caught up and blocked them.

Esther glared, her thickly lashed, light brown eyes cold, her chin raised haughtily. She asked, "*What* do *you* want?"

María put her hand on Esther's arm and smiled broadly at the man. "We were just waiting here to meet our friends so we can go to the park. If you want us to, we'll go wait somewhere else."

When María smiled, everything became brighter and the world would grow dark again when she stopped. No one wanted to refuse María, even though her nose was a bit large and slightly hooked.

The man waved them away. "Yeah, you girls go now! It's not safe for you to play here!"

The girls started to walk away, but after he went back into the clinic, they ran to the dumpster, knocked on it, and Esther rasped, "Get out of there, you *burros estúpidos*!"

Julian and Ricky stood up and began laughing, pushing each other back down into the trash by turns. Julian finally swung out, landing lightly on his feet. He was followed by Ricky, who resumed clucking like a chicken and dancing around while holding the inflated glove over his head.

María giggled.

"You almost got caught!" Esther scolded. "And you both stink!"

María said, "Hurry, before baldy-ugly comes back."

At that moment, a silver Lincoln Continental sped into the parking lot. The young friends watched wide-eyed and prepared to bolt. The Lincoln's oil pan clanged loudly against the gravel and the vehicle headed rapidly for them. The car swerved inches from their knees and parked. Momentarily frozen, they watched the woman driver, her silver earrings flashing, as she honked and shouted at them through the closed window. Hearts pounding, the youths ran off laughing. María squealed with delight. Julian risked a glance back and saw that the lady getting out of the car was wearing a white doctor's coat. *Qué loca doctora*, he thought.

At the bus stop, Julian imitated the crazy lady doctor. He made his mouth into a sharp parrot mouth, making reproachful soundless complaints to make them laugh. The four friends got on the same little orange bus that Ricky called El Cheapo, and each paid a few centavos. They sat as close together as they could in the crowded bus. Julian was very hot and sticky.

He said, "Let's go to the beach tomorrow…"

Ricky added, "and have a water fight." This comment was followed by a loud farting sound made by Ricky, using a rubber glove.

The girls began to plan a trip to the beach. Ricky punctuated their conversation with various rude sounds. He blew up the surgical gloves and then allowed the air to escape first through the wrist opening, and next through punctures he made in the fingertips for more excruciating, high-pitched noises. The yelps of disgust his female friends made and the approving glances of Julian encouraged him to continue despite disapproving frowns of several young mothers bouncing and patting their babies.

Julian held the syringes in his lap, his exploring fingers feeling the roughness of the broken, rough needles. A rancher carrying a crate of mangos edged by to get off. He jostled Julian, causing a syringe's tip to stab Julian's finger. He pressed his fingers together to smash the drop of blood that was forming like a balloon. Then he stuck his head out an open window. A breeze blew through his black hair, cooling his neck. He smiled happily while passing the striped umbrella-covered stands of venders who hawked beaded necklaces and gaudy visors. Children playing in the parks streamed before his eyes in a lazy parade. Julian listened to María and Esther talking about bringing horchata and burritos to the beach and thought, *Oh good. Mama would have told me to pack my own picnic.* He couldn't wait to fill the syringes with cold water. He thought, *I'll just have to be careful.*

At ten o' clock the next morning it was already hot and humid – a good day for the beach. The hot, heavy, Mexican air seemed to crush the men who worked alongside the cobbled roads. It squeezed the water out of the bored women and children under the trees who were waiting like damp rags for a bus. As the four of them walked together, Julian smiled at Esther and María, who were beautiful with beaded sandals on their brown feet, and brightly colored, hand-made bikini's under their shirts. They carried horchata and burritos. At a stoplight, Julian wiggled his barefoot toes, and envied Ricky's expensive tennis shoes. Both boys wore only cut offs, showing Julian's muscled chest and thick legs and Ricky's smaller, but well-formed, lean frame.

They stopped walking at the top of a seven-hundred step brick stairway leading from the road down to the sand and gazed at the beach below. It was Saturday, and the foursome could see that many families were already on the beach. The boys playfully began to push one another lightly, as if to push each other down the cliff.

Esther shouted, "Stop it now!" but she was smiling. The boys obeyed her. The dirt was hot beneath Julian's feet, and he jumped to the cooler, shady bricks as he climbed down the stairs winding along the side of the hill. Esther watched Julian's muscular back and his wavy, black hair moving in the breeze as he descended the stairs ahead of her. María was babbling happily to Ricky.

When Julian stepped into the sand, it was hot on the surface but soft and cool just below. The waves were small, and their lapping sound was refreshing. All along the beach for at least a mile, families were sitting in the water, letting the waves come in and cool them. Grandmothers in long dresses, which they had hiked up to their thighs, were sitting in the sand. Fathers wore white, straw cowboy hats, white T-shirts, and jeans. Mothers generally were tending little children and babies. Few had brought blankets, or picnics. For most of these people, the beach was just a stop along the way to the market. The small children played with brightly colored balls and floating toys.

Ricky and Julian ran straight for the water and splashed right in. The girls laughed at them and smiled at each other like doting mothers with rascally little boys. After setting down their bundles and taking off sandals, the girls walked to the water in their T-shirts. They stood in it at waist level. The boys, of course, splashed and teased them. The girls called them names and splashed them back.

Later, the boys ran back up the beach and flopped directly in the sand, coating themselves like elephants having a dust bath. Both girls filled out their bathing suits in classical, sensuous beauty, but they never took off the oversize T-shirts they wore.

16

Their wet T-shirts clung to their bodies as they walked in stately manner back to their colorful towels. Julian stared at them, amazed. He grinned at Ricky, and raised the thick, black eyebrows, which framed his sparkling, brown eyes.

After soaking up sun for a while, Ricky opened a bottle of tepid water and drank, offering some to the others. Julian drank some, but the girls demurred, preferring to drink their mother's horchata, which was still cool because they had protected it from the sun. María passed around some burritos filled with pork she and her mother had cooked twice to make it soft.

After eating, Julian was satisfied. He unwrapped a bandana and took out the syringes. He gave half to Ricky, and they ran down to the water to fill them. The object of this game was to squirt the girls, who were getting dry, and didn't want to get wet again. The chase was on, with the girls screaming and laughing. The girls in return, dashed to the waves and scooped water in their hands to splash the boys. The soaking boys didn't mind in the least – though they pretended they did – so that the girls would enjoy their revenge and continue the game.

After awhile, Esther said she wanted to walk into town. Julian refilled the syringes with salty water and wrapped them back into the bandana. They trudged through the sand and climbed back up the stairs.

Soon they were strolling through the small plaza, past little shops that had no windows or signs, only open doors with merchandise spilling out onto the sidewalks. They saw a family who sold hammocks, sewing them there in their house. They passed a shop, painted grotesquely pink, selling ice cream to a crowd of mostly overweight mothers and children. Next to it, sprawled a store that was covered with so many children's clothes, it seemed as if it had sprouted bird's feathers.

The four friends strolled inside food stores with the raw meat in chilled open cases, like reused aquariums, and they stared at the purple and white octopus and bright yellow chicken's feet. All around, small repair shops with windows that had no glass in them seemed to be on every block. Julian was fascinated with those, and he studied the various kinds of machines, imagining how he would use them.

Esther bought four, frozen, fruit pops from a vendor with a little white refrigerator hooked up to a generator. They ate them slowly, licking the juice while they watched a tortilla factory's small machine stack up tortilla after tortilla. Very hot now that her clothes had dried, María wanted to sit in the shade, so the group walked toward their barrio. Ricky was just finishing off his drinking water, when Julian took out a hypodermic needle, and squirted him.

Ricky pleaded unfair, demanding a weapon. Julian continued to squirt Ricky until the other boy sulked, and pretended to ignore him. Julian laughed at him and gave him a few, then quickly dodged.

Ricky called, "You may as well come back here now, because I'm faster than you, Bigfoot!" The fastest runner in the school, he soon caught up with Julian and squirted him squarely in the face. Then María and Esther wanted to play, so Julian gave them each a few. The four of them shouted and chased each other alongside dirt roads, grass, and small houses with vegetable and flower gardens. A great field of grass beckoned them and each got a second round of hypodermics and chased each other, squirting small amounts of salt water, which felt refreshing when hit by a breeze.

The needles were soon emptied, and they looked for a place to refill them. There was a small lumber mill along the road, with high brick walls, where Julian and his father had worked. It had a small spigot at one corner.

Ricky turned on the spigot, and all four of them held the needles under the running water, drawing up the plunger to pull in the water. Julian's would not fill, so he backed away and crouched down over the syringe. He pulled the plunger to release it from the needle section. Something seemed to be jammed. Julian stared down at the syringe and pulled out the plunger slowly from behind. It slipped, and then stuck again. He pulled at it harder. Suddenly, the plunger came out with a pop, sending the syringe, needle first, into his eye.

Julian pulled it out, throwing down the needle. He clasped his other hand over his eye and howled in pain.

"Put water on the eye. Wash it," Esther said. She put her arm around him to herd him toward the water spigot.

"No!" Julian cried. He would not take his hand off his eye.

"You've got to!" María said.

She cupped water in her hand and Julian finally let her pour it over his eye.

"Let me see it." Ricky said.

Esther came close for a look, too.

Clear liquid and red blood oozed from the center of Julian's eye.

Ricky's mouth fell open, and he clutched at his stomach, afraid he would be overcome with nausea. He declared hoarsely, "Let's get him home!"

They left the needles, and walked Julian home. Ricky ran ahead to tell Julian's mother, Marisol. Esther and María held Julian and said reassuring words.

Julian cried, "Why do I do such stupid things?" He swore to keep himself from crying.

"You're going to be all right," María said.

Esther said, "Of course you will," but her eyes were wide with fear.

Ricky and Julian's mother were waiting near the front step. Ricky was shifting from one foot to the other. Marisol was ready with hot, wet, clean towels in her big pot, which was tucked under her arm. When Julian stood in front of her, she cried, "*¡Julito!* What have you done?"

She saw it was serious, so she pretended it wasn't. "Okay, now. I'll take care of your eye, and you will be all right.

"Thank-you children, for bringing him," she added, closing the door.

Marisol led Julian to the cot, and began placing the hot, steamy towels over his eye.

The friends waited a long time and then left, calling back to Julian, "Don't worry! We'll come back and see you tomorrow! Hope you feel better!"

After they walked awhile, María squinted at the sun and said to her companions, "It would be awful not to be able to see."

Neither answered her, so she turned to see tears streaming down Esther's face, and gleaming in Ricky's eyes. He was barely holding them in, but the effort was turning his face red. María began sobbing. The girls embraced each other and then Ricky.

CHAPTER 2 THE HOUSE CALL

Julian lay on one of the two beds in the room that served for everything except the kitchen and the bathroom. The larger bed that his mother and younger brother shared was hidden from view by a colorful striped blanket opposite the kitchen. There was no glass in the windows and the floor was concrete. An old wooden table stood in the kitchen and a small fire pit for cooking on hot days blackened the cement outside the front door. The water in the house came from the faucets. This luxury was a recent addition due to the generosity of Julian's benefactors in the United States, Alan and Lena. Marisol's hands trembled as she lifted the warm, moist towel. She wadded her skirt under her knees to protect them from the cement floor and tucked her long braid behind her.

"Now let Mama take a look at that eye, Julito."

Julian frowned at her, moaning while she pried his lids open to see the eye. The whites were deep red, and blood bubbled up from the center of his pupil. Marisol stifled a cry. She turned and called Enrique.

"Go fetch *La Vieja*!"

Enrique ran out the door.

Within thirty minutes, the old woman came bringing a lamp and a bright woven bag full of herbs, a pestle, mortar and some bottles. After looking Julian over and saying "Hmmm." She carefully chose several herbs, ground them in her mortar with pure

22

water, soaked a clean cloth with it, and applied it to Julian's eye. This hurt and he cried out. Enrique gaped and clutched at his mother's skirt. *La Vieja* shushed Julian and bandaged him quickly. Julian rolled to his side and relaxed.

The old woman poured the rest into a bottle and gave it to Marisol, who paid her a few pesos. Then Julian went to sleep. Enrique began to ask questions, so Marisol explained simply that Julian had hurt his eye and needed rest in order to get better, so he had to be quiet. After a quick dinner, she laid the young boy next to the sleeping Julian. Later, Marisol sat by their sleeping figures and sipped some tea, staring at the darkness. Then, she lay down with them, her arm across both sons.

The next day, Julian insisted on going to school. If he didn't, he explained to his mother, he might not be able to stay at the top of his class.

Marisol watched him disappear into the streets, looking like a full-grown man. *Look at him*, she thought, *so determined to go.* She thought back to when the American couple had begun to help Julian, herself, and Enrique two years earlier. It was soon after his father's death that Julian had to quit going to school because Marisol couldn't afford shoes for his quickly growing feet. Julian began going out to the factory each day to sweep it out for a few dozen pesos. He had been eleven and taller than his former classmates and he said, "It's okay Mama, I'm big enough to go to work now. Don't cry." If Julian never got past sixth grade, it was no shame to most of the people they knew.

Julian's father had come down with a strange and sudden illness soon after he had accidentally killed his daughter. It was speculated by the townspeople that his sorrow and guilt combined had pulled him down to his grave. Some thought he had been cursed by an evil eye, perhaps by some jealous man. Julian was in fourth grade when he saw his sister killed, and he was in fifth grade when his father passed away.

The morning of the accident had been pretty much like any other, except that for an entire week, orders for rosewood had decreased. Julian's father had been working extra hard to avoid being laid off. It was 1994 and his pesos only bought of fraction of what he could buy before. In addition, there was violence in Chiapas and worse, a week earlier on March 23, 1994, the presidential candidate Luis Donaldo Colosio was shot and killed while campaigning in Tijuana. Julian's father absolutely hated President Carlos Salinas de Gortari. He was convinced that the president was involved with the crime bosses.

Julian watched his father get into the white, work truck. He continued to play in the tall grass with his handmade, toy truck, made out of tin cans, in the miniature dirt roads and tunnels he had carved out a week before. He could see his sister sitting in the driveway, in her yellow, plastic Big Wheel.

His father looked back over his shoulder, and waved to Julian. The back-up lights came on. His sister bent over to pick up a toy and sat up again. The truck backed up quickly. The rear of the truck bed smacked her head, slamming her and the Big Wheel over onto the concrete. The truck stopped. Julian's father jumped out of the truck's door, and rushed to her, crying out, "*¡Mija!*" He cried for his wife, who ran out, carrying her baby.

The girl's head was crushed on both sides and deep red blood ran down the long black strands of hair. She never opened her eyes or spoke again.

Julian was frozen in place in the grass and dirt with his toy truck for a long time, unwilling or unable to move until his mother's calls for him at last pierced his shock.

Six months later, her husband became extremely ill for the first time in his life. He ate rarely and only sipped a little chicken or tortilla soup when his wife begged him to. His hollowed eyes reflected both the death that he alone had caused and the death he now craved for himself. His family forgave him, wept with him, and pleaded with him to forgive himself. "We need you, Papa," Julian would say. "Don't die!"

Marisol had scolded Julian for saying that. "Of course he won't die," she said smiling bravely. "It was only an accident, my love," she would say. She begged the priest to come and speak to him.

"Her soul is in heaven now with the angels." the priest said.

"You must eat more and take walks in the sun," the doctor said.

His father's hands trembled and his feet shuffled. The once strong and confident man became weak and unsure of everything. His starved body had little resistance to bacteria in the water, bringing on severe diarrhea and dehydration. He died within a year of his daughter.

Marisol now worried about Julian. He had only recently resumed being a happy boy. She thought, *I must thank God for the kind Americans who send money so my son can return to school.*

She turned to her statue of Mary next to the mirror above a dresser. She forced herself to say a prayer of thanks to the Lady of Guadalupe, the kind mother of the Lord Jesus. Her plaster image was serene, her robed body and head surrounded by rays of wisdom and flowers. She prayed for Julian and lit a candle in front of the Lady of Guadalupe's statue.

Afterwards, she cleaned up bits of tortillas and scraped the rice cereal from the boys' breakfast bowls. Then she stepped outside and fed the scraps to a curly-haired neighborhood dog, and patted its head absently.

The next morning, when Julian lay in bed after awakening, throbbing pain made getting up for school unwelcome. He thought, *Maybe where father and sister dwell now, there are no more problems.* He imagined Heaven to be a meadow of tall white, yellow, and purple flowers, with streams flowing by, and fruit trees growing everywhere.

He sighed, dressed. After breakfast with Enrique, he packed a bag of tortillas, green onions, papaya, lime and fresh cheese for each of them while his mother got ready for her workday. He tried to be patient with Enrique as he dawdled over his breakfast, but he threw the bag lunch he'd made at the little boy. "C'mon, you're going to make us late!" Julian shouted.

While his mother hugged and kissed Enrique to make him stop crying, Julian shrugged off her questions. "Mama, you worry too much. I'll be fine. No, it doesn't hurt," he lied. Then he took the bus with Enrique, and let the boy off at his school. Afterwards, he got on another bus to his own school. He pressed his forehead against the bus window for its morning coolness.

In class, Julian had trouble seeing the board. He asked the boy in front of him, "What does it say?" and he wrote whatever his classmate said. A headache started, and got worse.

His teacher scolded him for whispering when he was asking his classmate what the teacher had written on the board.

Usually he spoke up in class and offered clear insights. He volunteered for jobs, or was playfully "volunteered" by his classmates and he would reluctantly comply with a smile. But now, he was very quiet. When asked about his swollen, red eye he simply said, "Oh, I scratched my eye. It'll be okay tomorrow."

During the next week, he couldn't do his homework. One day, he joined some kids who smoked cigarettes, and had one, thinking it might make him feel better. He coughed.

They laughed and slapped him on the back. One of the girls, wearing a blouse that left her shoulders bare, asked how he had hurt his eye. He was embarrassed and lied that it had happened in a fight.

In response, she touched his face, pressed against him, and said, "Aw...that's too bad."

Ricky, María, and Esther passed by. Julian was embarrassed and mumbled a hello.

The following week, he cut a class, sat by the railroad tracks, and threw rocks. He also played with a switchblade he got from one of his new friends. He carved a cross into the inside of his arm. The pain and the sight of blood dripping out were a relief compared to his heartache for missing his father, sister, and the pain in his eye.

Eventually, his teachers began to notice his flat affect, and apathetic demeanor, but Julian always brushed off their questions.

One morning, Julian wrote a note while Enrique was slowly eating breakfast. His mother had left to clean a large house and prepare fancy brunch for some rich old lady. He left the note by Marisol's statue of the Virgin.

Dear Mama,

I am sorry for all of the pain and trouble I caused you. I don't know why I am so stupid and do so many dumb things. It is just my choice to end my life, so don't feel bad for me. Tell my friends that I'm sorry, if they still care after the way I've ignored them. I want to be with Dad. If there is nothing after this life, that's fine, too. If I go to Hell, I don't care. I love you.

Julian then packed a lunch for Enrique and took him to school. He gave his brother a hug.

His brother stared at him.

Then Julian gave his brother some advice. "You be good in school okay? Mind Mama. I love you."

Enrique kept turning around to look at him as he walked to his class. Julian waved and smiled.

After getting off the bus near his school, he went to a store. He got an old man to buy him two bottles of whiskey. He went back to the railroad tracks with his knife and the whiskey. He watched a graffiti-covered train roar by. He wanted to get on one of those trains, but they sure went by fast. He drank all of the whiskey. It tasted horrible and burned all of the way down to his stomach, but he welcomed the feeling. He experimentally carved more lines into his arm for a while. Then he wondered if he should hop on the next train or just throw himself in front of it.

Marisol came home, dropped her things in a heap by the bed she shared with Enrique, and slid off her shoes. Her next job wasn't until 1pm and it was 11am. She spied the note by the statue of the Virgin and read it. She cried, "Oh my God!"

She ran to the school as best she could, unaccustomed to that form of exercise, as she was, holding her shoulder bag down to keep it from banging at her side. She darted across streets, deaf and blind to the honking and swerving of the cars around her. Another mother in the neighborhood stopped her car and drove Marisol to the high school.

The assistant principal, when he was summoned to the office, listened with a puckered forehead. After loosening his tie, he strode about the halls, while straining for breath. He pulled some students out of their classes to ask them where Julian had gone.

At last, a bare shouldered girl with penciled eyebrows said, "Well, sometimes he's at the railroad tracks by that road behind the school."

The assistant principal and Marisol hurriedly got in his car. They drove slowly, Marisol calling out his name and getting out to look down the tracks at a few places. When she found Julian, she ran to him, and hugged him tightly. Julian wrapped his arms around his mother, profound relief flooding through his body.

Kissing the top of his head, she said, "Thank God, I've found you, *mijo!*"

The train Julian had been awaiting roared by, blowing gravel on them both, and whipping Marisol's skirts. Hearing the tremendous clacking of the train's wheels, while in his mother's embrace, he decided that he had to live, if only for her.

When she got him home, she found that he had a high fever. She went to a couple of neighbors' houses to ask to use their phone. The operator connected her call to an eye clinic in Puerto Vallarta. Upon hearing the mother's frantic description, a doctor agreed to come take a look.

When the doctor finally arrived, it was 5pm, after the clinic had closed. She came in her silver Lincoln, speeding up the cobblestone streets of Puerto Vallarta and the dirt streets of the outlying village. Dogs, chickens, and children scooted out of her path. Dr. Bella jerked up the emergency brake, and reached over for her black bag. Hearing the brakes, Marisol sent Enrique out to bring the doctor into their house.

Julian, who lay upon a bed, saw through his good eye that the doctor was the same woman who had yelled at him and his friends in the parking lot. *Oh no. Not her*, he thought.

She had long black hair, pulled back in a loose ponytail, and large, silver earrings. She said, "What have you done to yourself?" Then she pulled a flashlight out of her bag, and examined his eye.

Julian had trouble relaxing. She then set the light aside for a moment to pull on a headband with an attached magnifying lens that she positioned over her eye, and looked again.

She turned and said to Marisol, "His lens is infected. You must let me remove it."

"How can this be done?" Julian's mother asked.

"I can do it right now for 1,000 American dollars. It sounds like a lot, but it's $2,000 in the clinic. You don't have insurance do you?"

Marisol shook her head.

"I know you don't have the cash now, but you can pay me when you can."

Marisol was shocked. This was about two month's wages. She remembered her manners. This was a special favor. Marisol was grateful, but she clasped the crucifix to her throat with both hands.

In the clinic, such an accident and infection would be partly paid for by the state, so the cost to Marisol wouldn't have been much different, but she wasn't about to doubt the doctor's word. Dr. Bella was the specialist.

Marisol watched Julian on the bed, his hand over his eye, and nodded, "Okay. Thank you so very much for making this special trip out here."

"I'm just dedicated to my work. Now, bring all the lamps you have into this room, near the bed here, and put turn them all on."

On a table she pulled over, she spread her sharp instruments out in their case. The low table had an embroidered cloth over it that now gleamed with scalpels, tweezers, vials of antibiotics, and antiseptics. More equipment clinked in the black bag as Dr. Bella pulled out sterile towels wrapped in paper, sealed bandages and another piece of headgear. This one had a bright lamp on the front.

To Marisol, Dr. Bella said, "You will have to hold his head very still while I administer the shot and perform the surgery. Be ready to wipe around his eye and don't faint."

Marisol whispered hoarsely to a frightened Enrique, who was standing on one foot and holding onto the kitchen doorway, "Go to the Romero's house tonight."

Dr. Bella said to Julian, "This shot will make it so you don't feel pain. The shot will sting a bit."

Julian held in his pain; another needle near his eye. He wanted to be brave.

He wouldn't show fear. He clenched his jaw, and the muscles in his cheek showed. The cords in his neck stood out. His mother petted his hair softly.

The doctor put the syringe down, and then she said, "We have to wait a few minutes. There are some important rules to be followed during the surgery, Julian. You must look straight ahead. Look at the window, and do not look to the right or left at all. Understand? Do not nod your head. Speak up if it hurts, but do not pull away. Do not focus on what I am doing. And do not stop staring at the flower in the window."

Dr. Bella looked at the lens one more time with a curling lip and a "tch" sound escaped through her lips. "This lens is perfectly worthless now."

Julian didn't dare nod his head or speak. The scalpel was inches from his face. Dr. Bella's incisions didn't actually hurt. However, if not for the desire to appear brave in front of his mother, he would have fought her like that last wild Mexican wolf with his paw caught in a trap, *El Lobo,* which his mother told him about. His mother's hands felt warm against his cheek and head as she held it still.

The doctor put her instruments down and bandaged the eye, after covering it with a white patch. She left ample pain pills and bandages with his mother, and directed the mother to change the patch daily.

Julian went to sleep and awoke with the patch over his eye. He accepted his injury with resignation. Days later when the patch came off, he encountered the repeated inconvenience of missing steps and grasping handles only to miss them. He certainly would not be safe working in a lumberyard like his father had. He thought, *I won't even be able to work in the lumber mill.*

At the end of each day, his head throbbed from worry and eye strain. His left eye was blind. His father and sister had died. He felt sorry for himself.

His father had been respected at work and in the town. He had been insistent that Julian work hard in school, and had taught himself whatever Julian was learning in school. His father had not completed fifth grade, but he was determined that Julian should do better.

Now, why should I care about school? Julian wondered.

A gun is the quickest way to kill oneself. The body hasn't long to fight to stay alive. It cannot force one to live while his soul is dead, once the bullet goes through the brain.

Who has a gun? He wondered. Esther's father and brothers have guns for killing cattle and for hunting, but they are too long to shoot oneself with. The only people who would have pistols are Javier Neri and his bodyguards.

CHAPTER 3
MARISOL'S SOLUTION

Julian slumped around the house, barely eating and rarely smiling. He was becoming more irritable and impatient with Enrique. Marisol shared her son's depression. God had stolen her daughter, then her husband, and now He was taking her son, too. There was nothing left that she could say to him that she hadn't said already.

But perhaps there was something she could do; give him the comfort of his friends. School was almost out for the summer, and Julian had recently stopped doing any work there at all. This complete lack of interest in learning – in anything – she recognized all too well.

She remembered how when her husband died, his former employer, Manuel, and his family, began to help. Meanwhile, she took in laundry, cleaned houses, and cooked delicately spiced meals for tourists staying in Puerta Vallarta guesthouses. Her sisters were happy to take care of Enrique. Julian went to school, did chores and took care of himself. That year, however, the 1994-95 peso crash had dried up most people's money. Wages and hours for her services, were to be cut still further. Mexico's costly bank rescue had only worsened the economy.

To help Marisol's family, Manuel hired Julian to sweep the factory floors and do general cleanup jobs after school. This had helped for awhile, but Marisol could not buy enough shoes for Julian, whose feet seemingly grew a size every month.

When he came to school barefooted, Julian was admonished that all students must wear shoes in school, and sent home. "Go home and get your shoes, and then come back," they said. Since he didn't have any shoes that fit, he simply did not go back.

Orders for rosewood continued to trickle in slowly at the factory and even Manuel had to find more work for himself, so he took a second job. He also maintained the properties of rich foreigner's houses in Conches Chinas. He never laid off a man. His wife, Audrey, opened a store and sold T-shirts and children's clothes. Due to the busy schedule Manuel's family was keeping, and due also to the pride and good manners of Julian and his mother, it went unnoticed for several months that Julian was sweeping out the factory earlier and earlier, when he should have been in school.

One morning, Manuel stopped the band saw when he noticed Julian sweeping sawdust at 11am, "Haven't you been going to school, Julian?"

"No sir. I only work now, to help the family have money."

Manuel remembered Julian's father: stubborn, intelligent, hard working, and anxious to learn. He was mostly self-taught and he had told Manuel proudly that his son was smart and would stay in school.

"Good idea. You're doing a fine job," Manuel smiled at Julian. Manuel's grief returned for Julian's father, who had been his most reliable and intelligent worker. He thought, *Julian must return to school somehow.*

Manuel told Audrey about the situation. She in turn, called her mother and father in the United States, and told them the story. Her parents, Alan and Lena Todd, discussed Julian over vodka and tonics for several nights. They had met Julian's father only once, but Julian was a friend of Ricky's, their grandson, and Audrey seemed very upset.

They began to send money so that Julian could attend school. Later, Julian became one of the top students. Alan and Lena, Audrey and Manuel had been like extended family to Marisol ever since that time.

Marisol took a break and walked to a nearby phone booth. She had planned this phone call and her purse was heavy with change. She pictured Audrey, always so golden, like a goddess.

"Audrey knows something about everything!" She had boasted to her sisters and friends. Marisol dialed and the operator came on. She asked for Audrey and said the numbers. Audrey answered cheerfully.

Marisol said, "It's me," and asked, "How is your husband? How is your son, Ricky?"

"Everything is going very well now," Audrey replied. "In fact, the way the economy is picking up, we were able to buy a wonderful resort. You should take a vacation and come and see it."

"Thank you for the offer. I will think about that," she lied.

"How is Julian?" Audrey asked.

"I am so worried about him. I think he needs to see his friends more, but he just mopes around like an old grandmother. He's getting poor grades, too."

"Julian should come and have a little vacation!

"It's almost spring break, and we're going to work on the new resort. Audrey said. "I'm sure we can cheer Julian up."

And so it was decided. Julian packed his small backpack, and one of Manuel's workers came to pick him up in a white company truck. Julian's thick eyebrows rose and then came together in a frown; this used to be his father's truck, the truck that killed his sister.

During the ride, he shut off the sad thoughts and looked at the supplies in the truck bed that were going to be packed into the speedboat.

When he saw Ricky run up to him excitedly, he couldn't help but smile. Ricky opened the truck's door and practically pulled him out, slapping him on the back.

He said, "Glad you could make it, hermit crab!"

CHAPTER 4
CASA FELICE; A PRESENT OF TIME

Soon they were motoring away from the dock, and then, with a slight smile, Manuel let the motor go full throttle. The engine roared impressively. The cool wind blew Julian's hair straight back like arrows.

Ricky called out to Julian, "This is the fastest and best boat on the high seas!"

Julian grinned back.

The spray from the bow of the motorboat on the glittering surface of the sea splashed into their joyful faces. Manuel calmly controlled the engine in the back of the boat, changing the speed according to some inner knowledge unknown to Julian. The boat bounced off the rolling waves, each bounce bringing more spray, and more laughter from Julian.

The coastline was white sand beaches and palm trees. Green mountains stood above the water, which reflected them in the choppy waves alongside the wide, vivid blue sky. Over their right shoulders, the city of Puerto Vallarta receded like the bass drum of a song playing in a Volkswagen that was puttering away. Ahead, a small, white plantation, like some Hollywood set, came into view.

At the shore of Casa Felice, Manuel called out, "Jump out and bring her in, boys!" He shut off the engine and jumped out, too.

Grasping the boat, they sloshed through the cool, waist high water, and hauled it over the warm sand, up toward the house.

Audrey, in a long dress and bare feet strode rapidly toward them. Julian stopped to look at the house. He noticed its large brick patio, which was shaded by towering coconut trees and the forests behind it. Ricky's mother and Manuel kissed and hugged, and Manuel said something to her that made her laugh melodically. She was slender, pretty and blond. Julian supposed that was because she was from the *Estados Unidos*.

He tried not to stare when Audrey shouted to the men, "Put the boxes up the hill there by the house! No, *next* to the house, not in front!" He'd never heard a woman give orders to men before.

Julian turned away and shaded his eyes to see the resort. It was a mile-long beach with two functioning bungalows and many more in the process of being built. Unfinished adobe and concrete bunkers were staggered between banana and coconut trees.

Audrey called to Ricky, who hurried to his mother, and she wrapped her arm around him. After a pause in which she studied his face, she asked, "How have you been? I've missed you."

He blushed, smiled and said, "Fine Mom." He glanced at Julian, and then asked, "Can we go snorkeling?"

"First, help your father unpack the boat. Ask if he needs anything. And come back before sunset!"

In the water, Julian saw a school of yellow fish with blue stripes, and below him, in the mossy rocks, an eel. He put his head up to call to his friends, who burst above the water; their goggled faces lit up with delight. Together, they submerged to chase the eel, which wiggled away in a cloud of mud to hide in a small cave. Julian followed it; bumped his head on the rock, and swam to the surface. His friend hadn't noticed, but he remembered; *I have to be careful now that I've lost my depth perception.*

With fountains of splashes, the boys came up to the surface. A mock fight ensued, with Ricky trying to dunk Julian. Julian, the stronger, dunked Ricky and then swam to shore. The other chased him.

Many lazy days followed, circling like the butterflies around the mountain path they often hiked. For two weeks, amusements such as playing with the dogs, and gathering coconuts by climbing trees and throwing them down alternated with helping Manuel and his workers improve the facilities and cottages around the grounds. Sometimes they assisted Ricky's mother with the gardening around the fountains and by the footbridge over the river. Mostly, they fished and swam.

Relaxed and tired, the boys trudged up the beach and sprawled in the hammock, and on the bed and couch arranged around the back porch. The breeze blew through the living room, which was completely open to the beach in front, and to the mountains in back. They stayed there, laughing, talking about their day until dinner, which was fish, caught that day by Manuel. After dinner, they all played games under the lantern, long into the night. The waves beyond breathed in and out like the breath of one in deep slumber. After awhile, the boys felt ready to walk to their bungalow on the other side of the beach. Audrey gave them solar flashlights and they padded out onto the cool night sand barefooted.

Hundreds of white crabs scurried across the flashlight's path. Ricky hooted and he and Julian chased the crabs. This was their nightly ritual. They yelled to each other and chased about a hundred more crabs into the waves. A large, red crab, waving its oversized claw, stood its ground in front of Julian, defending its little burrow; the little macho. Julian smiled and lifted his flashlight. He saw the formerly smooth beach had erupted with countless craters; burrows, from which thousands of crabs were now scurrying as they did each night during the off-season. Tonight the crabs seemed like helpless and foolish people rushing this way and that. The bold red crab seemed to be a wise man, brave, yet futile in his smallness; one lone prophet.

"Hey, leave them alone now, Julian!" Ricky called. "Let's go to bed!"

Their white, stucco cottage appeared tucked into evening's blue quilt and was well lit in the rising moon's light. The cottage was open to the beach, with nothing to close but screens. The rooms were filled with the sounds of the waves washing the shore, and the beds were slightly damp. The tousled boys flopped onto their beds and Ricky quickly fell asleep, but Julian listened uneasily to the crabs scuttling across the porch and up the back door with clacking and scraping sounds. Julian felt like sand was in his eye. He rubbed it awhile then gave up and tried to sleep.

CHAPTER 5 MANUEL STEPS IN

When Julian woke up, his eye was crusted, weeping, and wouldn't open all the way. He rubbed it, and tried pulling on the lid. At breakfast, Ricky's mother asked him to stop touching his eye. "You'll make it worse. You were probably bitten by a spider. It happens a lot around here this time of year. We spray for spiders and scorpions every year. Guess we better do it soon."

This last comment was directed at Manuel, who gave a nod. The heavy lady who was helping Audrey in the kitchen rolled her eyes at this new invasion of her work schedule.

Manuel accepted two huge scoops of scrambled eggs from Audrey and reminded her, "You'll have to leave for a few days so our guys can spray. You ready to start packing?"

"Boys, start packing right after you eat. I don't have many guests coming, so I'll cancel the Campbell party. I'll arrange to get a doctor to look at his eye and call his mother."

"Yes. It's time I looked after the lumber business and our own house anyway. Someone's got to," Manuel grumbled.

The boys took almost no time to pack the shorts and sandals they wore. They piled into the aluminum motorboat with Manuel and he sped them home. He left Ricky at his Puerta Vallarta house with the maid and the gardener and drove Julian home.

Marisol's little house smelled of fresh, sweet corn tortillas and she wiped her hands on her apron as she let Julian and Manuel in.

Shortly after they entered, the barking of dogs, the scraping of rocks under tires, and the yanking of an emergency brake brought them rushing back outside. Manuel observed the tall doctor in dressy clothes, smoothing back her long black hair. He wondered where she had been, dressed up as she was. She slammed the door to her white Honda, turned, and seemed momentarily startled to have been watched. To Manuel, the doctor gave an impassive, "*Buenos días.*"

"*Buenas días,* Dr. Bella," Manuel replied. "It was very good of you to come so quickly on such short notice."

"I was just about to start working with the outpatients at the clinic, but my young eye patients are my priority."

"*Gracias*," Manuel said, stepping forward to shake her hand.

She smiled at Marisol, and said, "I understand there is another problem with your son's eye?"

To Julian she said, "How are you feeling?" But without waiting for an answer, she continued, "Let's go inside."

Once inside, she shined lights in his eye, held it open and examined it with a magnifying glass.

"The cornea is badly scratched and infected. It needs to be removed," she declared to Marisol and glanced at Manuel.

"It would be an expensive operation," she added, "but, I can let you pay it back gradually like before."

Marisol bowed slightly and said, "Yes. Thank you, thank you." She lowered her head as politely and serenely as any blessed Catholic saint while accepting this further bad news.

Manuel motioned for the doctor to step outside. "May I speak with you outside please?" Once they were outside, he gave her one of his big flashing smiles, thanked her for her time, and pressed a hundred and sixty pesos into her hand. He said, "The boy's mother needs time to think."

"You can't delay! It will only worsen, damaging his optic nerve, making it unlikely that he could wear a prosthetic."

"A what?"

"You know it as a 'glass eye'."

As soon as Dr. Bella's exhaust fumes announced her departure, Manuel opened the door, signaled for Marisol to also come outside, and shut the door. In a low voice he said, "Don't have any more to do with her. I am going to find you another doctor."

Marisol asked, "Why do you want to find another doctor? She is an eye specialist. She can't be wrong."

Manuel explained patiently, "If she removes his cornea, that means he will lose his entire eye. My father-in-law tells me that the American doctors can insert a new lens, so don't let this doctor do anything yet. Even the best doctors can be mistaken sometimes. It will not do any harm to be sure, if we hurry. I promise I will find another doctor before anything happens to make his eye worse."

Marisol agreed obediently.

At home, Manuel explained all this to Audrey, who listened while she busily slapped meat around on the counter and chopped it as if it deserved to be punished.

Audrey pushed the meat into a hot skillet, wiped her Mexican tiled countertop, and said thoughtfully, "No doctor around here is going to argue with her opinion. You know how they all stick together."

"We could look for another doctor in Guadalajara."

"All right. I'll call the hospital in Guadalajara tomorrow."

The next day, before going to open the shop, Audrey called the hospital. She decided to check if they knew Dr. Bella first. She was put on hold.

The receptionist returned and said, "Yes, she has a practice here, and an office in Puerto Vallarta. Would you like to make an appointment?"

"No, thank you," Audrey said, and hung up.

CHAPTER 6 MARÍA

Ricky wanted his young friend María to talk to, and maybe to touch – to kiss, or to hold her around her little waist. It had been a month or more since he'd seen her at the beach on the day of Julian's accident. The bougainvilleas in front of María's house were brilliant against the white adobe, and the cactuses looked cheerful surrounded by clay pots of nasturtiums and geraniums. María's mother, a chubby woman in a loose white dress with colorful embroidery, greeted Ricky with a wide white smile from her deep brown face.

"Is it all right if I visit María, Señora?"

"María might not want to see you, honey. She doesn't want to see her friends right now, she says."

Ricky paused, his mouth hanging open dumbly. Usually María's mother was very enthusiastic in her greetings to him. But then, he had never come by himself before. Maybe that was what was bothering her.

"Why not? Please ask her to come see me," he pleaded.

She turned inside the doorframe and called, "María, it's Ricky! Come say hello, *hija*. María, you can't hide forever. Your friends care for you." The mother disappeared and reappeared, pushing María toward the door. Then María stood sullenly in the doorway, head turned away from Ricky. She could be moody and obstinate at times, shutting other people out when she was upset.

49

He smiled and put his hand on her arm, "What's the matter, María?" Ricky said, "¿*Qué paso?*"

María turned to him a little. Long purple cuts extended above and below her eyes, stitched with messy black threads that did not belong on María's warm brown velvet face. Behind her long, thick eyelashes, her eyelids looked sunken and empty.

"Oh, no…"

She turned angrily toward him; both eyes were slits filled with shadows. The two stood in silence, each waiting for the other to speak. Suddenly, María slammed the door. The wooden door, roughened from the sun.

"María, come back! Open the door!" he called, but there was no answer. He could hear the mother asking María why she shut the door on her friend, but the door remained closed.

Ricky ran along the dirt road toward the house where their friend Esther lived. It was half a mile away.

Fences surrounded her house and these fences contained many obstacles: mainly older brothers, but also cattle, goats, rams, sheep, chickens, and barking dogs. Esther's window was on the second story. Pure white curtains drifted out the window in the breeze.

"Esther!" Ricky called to her windows, to her yard, to her barns.

Esther's smiling face appeared, "What, you cow's head?"

His shoulders stopped hunching up at the sight of her. He was breathing hard, "Please come talk to me, outside."

Her head ducked inside and shortly she appeared, her white shirt gleaming above her blue jeans, which were tightly stretched over her muscular legs. Her long, black hair slithered and waved around her narrow waist.

"What has happened to María, Esther?"

Her smile faded. Ricky felt weak, and he began to look for a place to sit. She frowned, looked around, and said, "Come on." She pulled him away from the house toward the far end of the corral, near the creek. They sat on the fence.

Esther began, "After you and Julian went away, María and I got bored, so we went south on the bus with my older brothers and sisters. They always get to go. Of course, they didn't want to take us at first. My brother's friend, Carl – remember him? Well, he met us with his truck and we piled in the back and went up to the water hole near Chico's Paradise. We were just swimming, playing on the rope swing and sliding down the rockslide. You know, just fooling around. Well, I was sliding down into the water from the rock when we all spotted a monkey coming down towards our things. We had them piled on a rock near the stream. I splashed down and when I crawled out onto the rocks, María was protecting our bags from the monkey. The monkey was getting too close and my brothers told her 'Get back!' and 'Don't worry about the bag.'

She was so stubborn; she wouldn't leave it alone! The monkey grabbed her bolsa and María grabbed it, too. Then, the monkey clawed her face! Several times. Turns out the stupid monkey was drunk. The bartender makes him Piña Coladas and banana drinks."

"Is she going to be all right?"

"The doctora from Vallarta said both eyes were cut up, and they could not be saved, so she took them both out!"

Ricky couldn't remember if he said good-by or if he walked Esther back to her house. He went home and tearfully called for his mother as he walked in. The maid answered and fetched Audrey. In the tiled kitchen, Ricky told her what he saw and what Esther had said. He waited for her reaction, perched on his chair, his green eyes wide.

Audrey repeated, "Oh my God!" several times. Manuel came and stood at the door, listening and frowning.

Later, Manuel discussed Ricky's story with his wife. This new development combined with the information that the Vallarta doctor was the eye specialist in Guadalajara made them feel it might be best to send Julian to the United States. Because Audrey's parents were American, Manuel and Audrey bought many of their goods in the United States to get quality merchandise. The same was true in medical care sometimes. Audrey had gone back to the United States when it was time for

Ricky's birth because she didn't want to walk in the fields with cows while in labor.

CHAPTER 7 MÍSTER MUSTACHE

The little children in Yelapa called Alan *"Bigotes"* because of his red mustache. Alan's mustache was similar to a *bigotes de foca*, or a walrus mustache. Manuel gave him that name when he had worked in the Yelapa hotel, while courting Alan's daughter whenever her family spent their holidays on Yelapa's beaches. These days, Manuel also called him *Suegro* (father in law). Now Alan sat at his antique desk, in his California mansion. Retired, he managed his money and property by phone in his office at home. When the phone rang, he immediately picked it up.

"Bigotes," Manuel's voice sounded clear for such a long distance call, "The doctor here wants to take Julian's eye out. She says that his cornea is too infected. This doctor also just removed both eyes from one of Ricky's schoolmates, too! I don't trust this doctor, but she's the only eye specialist for almost 200 miles. What do you think we should do?"

"Tell you what I'll do, Manuel. Can you pack him up, get him a passport and put him on a plane? I'll pay for the passport and the ticket." Alan rolled one of his Haitian, antique handmade toy trucks along his desk while he waited for Manuel to answer.

"Yes, I'll do it right away, *Suegro,* before you can forget what you said you'll do."

"You're a real funny guy, Manuel. I can't tell you how glad I am that my daughter married a Mexican comedian."

Manuel smiled and said, "*Bigotes,* don't tell Julian about the little girl that has lost her eyes. I think he will be very upset."

"I won't. I'll send you a check. Don't let that quack near him. I'll get him a decent doctor." He smiled and added, "After all the money I've invested in that boy, I'm not going to let anyone take his headlights out without a qualified second opinion."

The task of finding the birth certificate needed to fly Julian out of Mexico fell to Marisol. She rode back to Julian's first doctor's office, on the bus. It was a winding trip over mountains, followed by a mile-long walk. The small, dim office was crowded with mothers and their children, many of whom were wearing eye patches. Marisol recognized one of the mothers, a friend with a daughter Julian's age.

"*¿Qué pasó?*" Marisol called to her old acquaintance.

"*Es su ojo otra vez,*" (It's her eye again) the woman explained, "and I don't understand it, because we do what the doctor tells us but it keeps getting worse."

"Have you been seeing this doctor for her eye?" asked Marisol.

"No, another one in Puerto Vallarta. A woman. This doctor sent me to her."

"Did you see Dr. Bella?"

"Yes!" the woman said. "Our village seems to be having bad luck. So many of our children are losing their eyes."

"Maybe she is a bad doctor," said Marisol.

The other woman frowned and protested, "Our doctors are good people. It's our politicians and our police who are crooked."

"They may not be the only ones," Marisol said.

Marisol got a copy of Julian's birth certificate, and went out through the waiting room again. She scanned the faces, looking for her friend again. She must have been taken in to the office. Seeing the bandages on the children's eyes once more, her hand tightened protectively around her son's birth certificate. She hurried away down the dirt trail and impatiently rode the slow bus with its many stops at small farms and villages.

At last she arrived in Puerto Vallarta, and from a public phone in front of a general store on the highway, she called Audrey, "Can you help me apply for a passport for Julian, *por favor?* I don't want to go to the office by myself."

"Sure!" Audrey exclaimed, "How was your trip to your old doctor's?"

Marisol told her about the other mothers with children who had eye patches and about meeting her friend there.

"You know what? Let's just go take care of his passport tomorrow, at 1. I'll meet you at the government offices center, at the front by the flags. Bring Julian, his birth certificate, and his school attendance papers."

The next day, few workers seemed to be present in the dim green offices. Those who were there moved slowly and greeted them in a friendly but vague manner.

"Excuse me. Where can I get a passport for a thirteen year old boy to go to the United States for an operation?"

"*Aquí, Señorita,*" said a handsome young man with a thick black mustache.

Marisol gathered her son's birth certificate and school attendance papers from her woven bag.

"Fill out these forms," the man said.

Audrey helped Marisol fill out the many forms. Meanwhile, the man sat Julian at a booth and snapped his picture. Julian stared at the camera passively, and then wandered back over to his mother and stood close by her side. She struggled with reading the forms.

He took the pen from her and said, "I can fill out the rest, Mama. You sit down."

Marisol gave him a squeeze, "*Está bien, mi hijo.*"

Julian and Audrey finished and turned in the forms.

The man smiled flirtatiously at Audrey and said, "These forms will be processed and the passport will be ready for you to pick up in three months. Then you can come back and visit me again."

"You can't mean it. You can't be serious! He needs to be seen by a doctor in the United States right away!"

"Señorita, have patience; these things take time."

"He doesn't have the time!" Audrey cried. The man's face hardened. He shook his head and shrugged his shoulders.

"Will this help?" she asked, leaning over the counter and holding one hundred dollars worth of pesos out to him.

"*Sí*, Señora. It will be ready in a week."

A week and a half later, Audrey sped Julian over the cobblestone streets across town – jostling with the other cars over where the center of the road actually was, and walked him to the ticketing booth in the airport.

"Mr. and Mrs. Todd will meet you right at the gate when you get off the airplane in San Jose. Do you have their phone numbers, and your money?"

He showed them to her.

"Good. Now here is your passport, your ticket and more money."

The plane whined loudly as it matched its doors up to the tube-like passageway. The windows trembled with the roaring noise and Julian backed away like a horse rearing up when startled by a snake.

"Julian!" Audrey's thin hand grabbed his arm; her knuckles were like little white mountains. She pulled him into a hug. Her blue eyes twinkled kindly. "Don't be afraid! The airplane is just like a bus. I've ridden it many times."

Julian nodded as he listened, and he watched people filing out. The announcer called for passengers to start boarding.

She led him to the line that was forming, "We'll be waiting to hear from you and Alan as soon as you arrive. Tell him to call us. Don't worry. Manuel and I will watch out for your mom. Bye!"

She gave him another hug and then a little push toward the gate and the flight attendant. Julian walked into the tube.

At the airport in San Jose, California, the mustache of *Bigotes* was easy to find. There next to him in the white halo-like hat was Lena. Although Julian usually called Alan "*Bigotes*" when talking about him to Ricky, he now called him Mr. Todd. "*Hola, Señor Todd.*"

"Julian! How was your trip?" asked Alan, gripping Julian's hand with both of his.

Lena asked, "How do you like flying?"

Both of them were smiling so much that their faces twinkled. Alan's eyes looked like the ocean during a sunny holiday. Still, Julian was frightened, so he only mumbled, "*Es Bueno.*"

Mr. Todd had the large belly of a wealthy man, and Lena had the figure of a girl. She didn't seem old enough to be Audrey's mother.

The airport sounded like a traffic jam in a tunnel. The crowds looked like the tourists in the plaza shops in Mexico. Everywhere Julian looked, there were still more people.

Julian's stomach growled.

Mr. Todd said, "We'll get some food in you; then let you rest. You've got a couple of days until your appointment."

After arriving at an enormous house, Julian unpacked, ate, and rested. Later, they watched a movie. Julian had seen a movie on a VCR before at Ricky's house. This time they watched *The Addams Family*. Julian thought it was funny, and he liked the man who had a lightbulb in his mouth.

Wednesday morning, they drove through commuter traffic to a plain, white building. Doctor Fishman examined Julian's eye. It was no surprise to Alan and Lena when the doctor stated that Julian's inflamed cornea only needed some antibiotics. When Julian finished growing, the doctor said, he could even be fitted with an artificial lens; he would be able to see normally again.

The next morning, Alan was speaking on the phone to the local paper, "Look into the case of this doctor who is taking children's eyes and selling them. She took out an eye, and in some cases two eyes from eight children in a couple villages near and around Puerta Vallarta. There are more children around Guadalajara whose eyes she has taken out. She is the eye specialist for the hospital in Guadalajara."

"Sir, do you have any documentation?"

"All I know is what I've told you, and that the doctor here was able to save the eye that the doctor was going to remove."

"Well if you find out anything else that is for certain and is documented, give us another call."

Alan set the phone down gently, but swore, "Damn! No one wants to investigate this!"

Lena looked up from the plant she was watering, "Call your congressman," she said matter-of-factly.

"I think I will," he agreed.

Four days later, Alan received the message that his congressman, Tom Campbell, had notified the Mexican Embassy. Furthermore, the Mexican Embassy had notified the authorities in Puerto Vallarta.

CHAPTER 8 WORKING

Julian returned to the Puerto Vallarta Airport, smiling. Audrey met him, and then helped him collect his many bags and packages. They piled in the van with a new Nintendo 64, a television, a CD player, and CDs and games. Julian also arrived wearing stylish, new American clothes, and brought back with him several new outfits, including surfing shorts, bright Hawaiian shirts, sandals and sunglasses.

Audrey drove the black, hot, recently paved roads east, away from the coast of Puerto Vallarta, to where the homes often had chicken wire for windows and the yards were large. It was unclear where one property began and another ended, except for an occasional decaying fence. Factories, homes, warehouses and whorehouses cohabited chaotically. Julian's house, and a few around his were neatly painted, while most of the neighborhood's buildings had peeling paint concealed by shaggy, flowering plants.

Julian's mother and brother came running out of the little, white house into the dirt street, calling out happily to Julian. Marisol asked, "¡Hijo mio! ¿Como está? How are you my son?" She hugged him, and held him at arm's length, inspecting his face and eyes.

Audrey laughed and said, "He's just fine! He's been ogling every girl we've passed!"

"Speaking of important girls, how are *you* mama?" he asked her.

"I am perfectly fine. Please put your things in the house. I need to talk to Ricky's mother."

They watched Julian reach into the van and pull out the many items. He began balancing more boxes in his arms to carry.

After he was in the house, his mother turned to Audrey and said, "*¡No lo puedo creer!* I can't believe it! Where will we put it all? If your family keeps treating him like this, he will want to move into *una casa rica* on the hill with the mansions." She gestured toward the tourista area along the coast.

"*Pero, gracias Señora,* for all you have done." She smiled, finished with her scolding and said, "May God bless your father and mother for this miracle".

Enrique pulled on his mother's skirt, "If he does move to a mansion, mama, I'll stay with you!"

Audrey laughed, "I hope all of these things don't crowd you too much. If Julian needs any help setting up his things, Ricky will help him, and Manuel will come to check on the electrical connections for you. Don't worry about a thing. *¡Adios!*"

After Manuel went to Julian's home and put in additional electrical outlets, he complained to his wife, "*Los Suegros* (his in-laws) are spoiling Julian!"

"Yeah, but you love it, though," Audrey said.

The next day, Julian met Ricky's at a house that had its living room converted into screened-in diner. Under one of the Formica tables, a chicken wandered, looking for scraps. Above Ricky's head, an iguana climbed the chicken wire that served as a window. The owner's daughter served them lemonade and tortilla chips with salsa. A young man carrying a guitar came in and sat down. He leaned the guitar against the wall and called for a *cerveza*.

Julian ate the chips and drank lemonade as Ricky chatted. After a while, Ricky began to break chips in his hand, and grind them into a mess on the plastic tablecloth. He said, "I feel awful about what happened to María. I hate to tell you."

Julian leaned forward, "*¿Qué Pasó?*"

Ricky told him what had happened to María.

"I don't believe it! Don't joke around about María."

"I'm not joking. I wouldn't joke about this."

Julian's eyes stung with tears. His blood rushed to his ears and began to pound. "No! Both eyes?"

Ricky nodded. The guitar player stared at Julian.

"I want to stop that witch," Julian rasped. He held his fists rigidly alongside his thighs for a long while and looked out on the dirt road. He said a prayer, "Mother of God, have mercy on me. I hate that doctor."

"But the doctor only took out her eyes because of the damage the monkey did."

"Ricky, there was nothing wrong with my eye at all, and she wanted to take out my eye. I don't believe for a second that she needed to take out both of María's eyes. She shouldn't be allowed to take care of a dog!" After a resigned sigh, he asked, " Is María's mother taking care of her very well?"

"*Sí*, she is, but María never goes anywhere. Esther says that they can't afford the plastic eyes, and María is ashamed to go out. It's bad. I'm sorry to say that I was afraid of her when I saw her. Now she won't talk to me."

"What did you say?'

"I don't know. I was just shocked."

Julian nodded. The man at the nearby table began to strum a sweet, soft tune. What would his father want him to do for María, Julian wondered. "I *must* do something," he said. "I would have lost my eye, but *Gracias a Dios*, friends helped me. So I must help her."

Ricky bit his lip for a moment. Then he wiped a tear with the tail of his shirt.

Julian said, "I'll get a summer job to pay for María's eye replacements. I can work around the fishing and touring boats. Maybe Manuel's brother will give me a job."

Ricky nodded, his eyes lighting up and his gaze lingering on his friend's face, "*¡Qué buena idea!* I want to help, too! Why don't we go, now and ask my Dad?"

The boys abruptly got up from the table, the wooden chairs scraping the cement floor. Ricky called, "¡*Adios!*" to the cook who was flattening beans and mixing them with lard in a skillet. She smiled and waved a spoon at him.

As they walked the dusty road to Manuel's factory, the boys heard whine of the saws cutting rosewood boards. Next, they opened the twelve-foot tall iron gate and passed men cutting boards on a huge circular saw. The fresh wood shaving's fragrance made Julian realize that he had been breathing dirt, sage, and a bit of manure for what seemed forever. Then the boys stepped into Manuel's small, plain office. Manuel sat writing at a black steel desk which dominated the room. His eyebrows shot up when he recognized them.

"Nice to see you, boys. So Ricky, do you want to sweep sawdust? I'll pay you. My former helper here seems to be too busy these days," he teased.

Julian laughed, "Good idea Manuel. I will help too, if you pay me more than you used to!"

Manuel laughed.

Ricky said, "No, really Dad, would you ask your brother to give us a job, *por favor?*"

"Oh, so you want a more generous employer now? *¿Por qué?* You want to take girls out on expensive dates?"

Julian smiled and blushed, but then set his jaw firmly and said, "No. It's for something important."

Ricky spoke up, "He wants to do something really nice for someone, but doesn't want to say what yet, in case he can't do it, I think."

Julian gave Ricky a little shove.

Manuel had an instinctive feeling about what Julian's idea might center around and understood. He made the phone call from the sturdy black phone at his desk. As he spoke, he made faces at the boys and smiled. "You're right," Manuel said into the receiver, "he hasn't worked since *Bigotes* bought him shoes and sent him back to school. Well, if he acts lazy I will take away his shoes. *Sí. ¡De acuerdo!* (It's agreed.)"

"But Dad, what about me?" Ricky complained.

"You can start being more helpful to your mother."

The next morning, Julian went to the docks to look for Javier Neri, Manuel's older brother, although he was unsure which boat it was and what Javier looked like. The dock creaked with every step, and seagulls fluttered out of the way, squawking at Julian. Waves crashed noisily into the rocky shore, while Julian scanned the harbor's blue and white swaying boats. An engine started up, its exhaust burbling into the water. Men were throwing lines onto the boat.

Julian cupped his hands around his mouth and yelled above the din, "Do you need a helper to cut bait, clean fish or hook bait? Is this Javier Neri's boat?"

The men shook their heads no and the boat chugged away. Across the dock, a man in a straw hat called his name. He reached out and helped Julian up into the boat. It was large enough for a forty-person party or a twenty-man fishing crew with gear and vats or live wells for the caught fish. The boat was tall; a large cockpit sat above several staterooms and a wide deck. Javier was dressed like an ordinary fisherman, with his tattered, yellowing T-shirt. Julian had imagined him to look more elegant, like the other man, since Javier was a lottery winner – a multimillionaire.

Javier said, "Julian, it's good to meet you at last. Your timing is perfect because I need another strong, responsible worker. Boat needs to be scrubbed top to bottom. Supplies are in the cabin. The toilet needs to be swilled too. If you're any good, you can help restock the boat for its next trip."

Julian nodded and began looking around the boat. Then he heard the clumping of feet beneath the deck and saw a door slide open. Two men emerged from the cabin, accompanied by the smell of cigar smoke. A tall, heavy, but muscular man wearing a crisp, white shirt and pressed khaki pants carried a drink in one hand and a cigar in the other. He strode across the deck, the ice cubes in his drink rattling as the glass tipped this way and that precariously. His eyes appeared to be laughing as he gazed at Julian, his mouth half-smiling. The younger man had a muscular build and a thick neck. He stared at Julian without smiling. They both stood next to Javier.

Javier gestured toward the well-dressed man and said, "This is Victor, *mi amigo*, and this young man here, is my bodyguard, Pedro."

Julian was stunned into silence, and the men laughed at his discomfiture. Julian then laughed, too.

"*Pues*, get to work, Julian. Just find the scrub brushes, soap and bucket below deck. Scrub everything and then oil down the wood. See that you close and lock the cabin. If you finish before we get back, come back early in the morning, tomorrow. Show him where things are and how to do it, Pedro. *¡Pronto!*"

Afterwards, the men swung themselves out of the boat and strolled up the dock towards the road. Julian went down into the cabin and gathered sponges, soap, a mop, rags, and oil for the teak wood trim inside. He took the bucket to the little sink, and tried to fill it but the sink was too small, so he jumped off the boat and filled the bucket with water from a nearby spigot. He hefted the bucket back on the boat and climbed aboard. He began at the prow with the sponge, soap and bucket, scrubbing salt and mildew off the boat. The back of his neck tingled and he looked up to see that he was being watched by several other boat owners or their helpers who resumed cleaning their boats when they saw him staring back at them. Julian wished that Ricky had been allowed to work with him.

The next morning, Javier met Julian on the docks. "*¡Buenos Dios* Julian! Good job. She shines proudly, ready to take you on a date, if you want to come with us later."

The early sun made golden sparkles on the waves and white-blue radiance emanated from the boat, lighting up Javier's face. "It's your second day on the job, so it's time for the important job: getting the beer! But first, how to empty boat's toilets."

Javier showed him the tubes that emptied the toilet's storage tank, the connection to a septic tank on the dock and the switch, which ran the pump. Julian mixed chemicals the way Javier directed and added them to the toilet's storage tank.

"Now let's see how you shop. You take this money and list, then go to the Mercado Real, on Camino Soledad. You know the place? Here is a note explaining that it is I who request the Coronas. Then you come back here on the bus. Be quick about it, eh? You still want to go with us for a boat ride?"

Everything sounded great to Julian. He nearly ran to the little bus stop and waited impatiently for the bus. Soon he was rushing about the market gathering a full basket and finally, the beer. The clerk read Javier's note with a nod, looked closely at Julian, and handed him two bags.

Julian made long strides across the dock soon after, and the two men who had been there the day before were assembled onboard the boat with two ladies and Javier. Both ladies were pretty, wore expensive clothing, hats and sunglasses. One seemed to be about his mother's age, but the other, she looked like a ripe mango.

Javier said, "This is my wife, Señora Neri, and Victor's lady, Señorita Rita. Ready for a boat ride?"

"Pleased to meet you both, Señora and Señorita," Julian said shyly.

When Rita took a bag from him and squeezed it to her chest, the tops of her breasts bulged, creamy and smooth. As she passed by him, Victor gave her bottom a playful swat. Then, Señora Neri took the other bag from Julian, and both women went below decks. Javier climbed up the ladder to the large cockpit at the top, started the motor, and grabbed the wheel. Pedro jumped off the boat and freed it from its moorings. He jumped back on as Javier began motoring away from the dock. The bodyguard and Julian stood on the deck, holding the rails, while Victor prepared the rods and tackle in a leisurely way. The bay was enormous and deep blue. Beneath the water, large, brown turtles were swimming.

Victor followed Julian's gaze and said, "Those are sea turtles. Ay, it is good to be out here again. Javier doesn't have to fish for a living now that he won the lottery, but he still enjoys it. Do you enjoy fishing, Julian?"

71

"It's okay, because I like to be able to help supply food to my mother and my family."

"So, that's why you were looking for work?"

"No. There is a girl who needs money.

"Did you get her pregnant?" asked Victor, setting the baited poles into some holders.

"No," said Julian, and he explained what happened to both María and himself.

Victor took a sip of his drink, wiped his lip with the back of his knuckle and continued to rub his lip thoughtfully, "Doctors make good money, but that one must have some special skill. She's got more than five houses in Puerto Vallarta alone. She's very clever."

"She is a very bad doctor!" exclaimed Julian.

"You've got an interesting story, but it's hard to believe it about a doctor who has it made. Especially her, she is a specialist – a popular one."

"Who is hungry?" Señora Neri called out as she stepped out of the cabin.

She carried a tray of drinks and Rita carried two trays of crackers, bread, olives, caviar, cerviche, smoked fish, cheeses and fruit. Julian forced himself not to stare at Rita and looked at the food instead. Señora Neri handed Julian a Coke from the tray, "*Aquí.* Is something the matter? Aren't you hungry?"

Julian looked at her, "I'm fine. *Gracias.* I've just never been on such a big boat before, Señora...."

Suddenly, they had to hold on to their plates of food as wind began blowing when Javier sped up and cruised at thirty knots.

"Slow down, Javier, or we'll lose our food!" Señora Neri called.

Javier gave her an irritated look, and slowed down just the slightest bit.

Victor laughed and he and Pedro grabbed a large piece of smoked fish each. "We must not lose any of this wonderful lunch you ladies made. Better eat quickly everyone!"

Some crackers sailed over the edge of the boat. Seagulls swooped down as if they had seen this all coming and made off with round morsels in their bills. The boat soared into the air over the swells. Water splashed them hard in their faces. Señora Neri hunched protectively over the cerviche and smoked fish, "I'm sorry he is going so fast."

"Don't worry – this is fun, isn't it Julian?" Victor said.

Julian's white smile shown more brightly because of a newly acquired deep tan, and his hair hung down longer than usual, dripping water.

Finally, Javier cut the engines and joined them. Although everyone but Javier was soaked, no one complained. Everyone finished eating, and only Javier and Victor were still drinking, as they would throughout the trip. The two men set Julian up with a fishing pole, tackle, and bait. The pole was larger than what Julian used when he caught fish for his mother to cook for dinner, but he hooked the bait onto the line and cast. Sometime later, the pole was almost yanked out of his hands.

"Hold on. You've got one!" Victor shouted.

Javier said, "It's a Striped Marlin."

The giant fish fought with mighty thrashings, its sword cutting in all directions. Julian pulled till his shoulders ached while everyone cheered him on, "You've got him! Don't let go! Reel it in quickly, before he cuts the line!"

Julian, leaning back, his feet spread apart, he fought at times against the fish, which seemed to be trying to pull him into the sea. Exhilarated and relieved, he at last brought the great fish to the floor of the boat with a resounding thump. The women yelled excitedly and headed for the cabin, and peeked out to watch this war between men and fish. The fish leapt and jabbed wildly. Victor leaned over with a large gaff and tried to hook it in the gills. The bodyguard fetched and swung a rifle at the fish's frightening head and cracked its skull.

"You shouldn't have brought that rifle out!" shouted Javier at Pedro. "You could have used something else. You can't just be pulling the guns out any time you need to fight something. Go put that away."

Victor drawled, "Hey! Take it easy. The boy isn't worried about the gun. He's just happy that the swordfish is ready to be cut into pieces instead of it cutting him into pieces."

He turned and explained to Julian, while winking at the adults, "That rifle is in case of pirates. This is the first time we've actually needed it on board!"

The ladies laughed appreciatively and Señorita Rita wrapped her arm around Victor. He squeezed her affectionately.

Javier grunted and pulled a pocketknife out of his pants pocket. He opened it and handed it to Julian. "Let's see how you clean fish. Take it to the prow and see that you don't drop the knife."

When they arrived back at the dock, Javier had Julian divide up the cleaned fish three ways, nine pounds of fish each. Julian's share was wrapped in newspaper. As he was turning to go, Javier stopped him and gave him 360 pesos, the equivalent of forty dollars American money. Julian stuttered, "Thank you," and stared at Javier. This was too much money for the little that he did, plus all of the fish that he received. It would go a long way toward making the payments for María's eyes, though. "When can I work for you again, Señor Neri?"

"On Monday morning, wash this boat and then come to the address on this card," Javier said, "I've got plenty of jobs for a good worker like you."

Julian remembered that Javier was generous. He had heard his mother and Ricky's mother criticize him for throwing his money around, drawing attention to himself and his new wealth.

In the morning, Julian hosed the boat down; careful to get all of the salt water off, like Javier had warned him. He tidied the boat and scrubbed the fish guts from the prow. It was cool and pleasant work, that is, until he had to clean out the sewage tank. Afterwards, Julian took the bus to the base of the mountain road where the rich people's fortress-like houses were. He hiked up the cobble stone street in the heat and humidity, which felt like a smothering wet blanket. After a two mile hike and some aimless and thirsty searching, Julian found the house by asking all of the servants, gardeners, and workmen in the neighborhood where Javier Neri lived. They pointed and said, "Farther up the hill."

The front drive of the highest house was a mess of wet cement, bricks and scurrying hod carriers. They confirmed that Señor Neri lived there. He knocked at the door of what appeared to him like a castle. A servant girl in a starched, plain dress answered. She called over her shoulder, and another woman came to the door. She was apparently the cook, for she was wearing an apron and wiping her hands on a dishtowel. This older woman asked Julian many questions and then let him in. She took him to the kitchen and gave him a cold rice drink, spiced with nutmeg, and a tortilla filled with steak, avocado, and salsa.

She spoke gently and rapidly. "You are to work with the gardeners. Señor Neri and Señora Neri are out, but you will meet his chief gardener and help him put in new plants. You will see Señor Neri Friday if you last the week. Did you get enough to eat?"

Julian nodded enthusiastically while chewing.

The cook smiled like a sweet grandmother, then turned from him and bellowed through the open back door, "Juan! The young worker is here!" Then she gave Julian a large jar of ice water. "Be sure to drink this while you work. Oh, and there is an outhouse in the back of the yard."

Juan had a big, square, friendly face and wore a cowboy hat. He asked if Julian was ready for some hard work, and took him to the back garden where two men were groundbreaking and shoveling deep holes. Nearby, there were about fifteen large trees in the yard in square crates. Juan took Julian to a patch of dirt and outlined a five-foot square area and told Julian to dig down four feet. He gave Julian a large pickaxe and a shovel. Julian started swinging. The ground was harder than he expected; it seemed to be mostly rocks. After a while, he got a rhythm to his work, swinging the sharp tool, breaking the ground, and pulling out the rocks. When he'd put down the pickaxe, he shoveled the dirt out to the sides, and it strangely satisfied him to see the large piles of dirt that he had wrestled out of the ground. When at last the hole was large enough, Juan gave him a wire screen and a wheelbarrow to sort the rocks out of the soil. He put a few shovels full of dirt on the screen, rattled the screen back and forth until only fine soil was in the wheelbarrow and all sizes of rocks were left on his screen. These he chucked into a large pile. It grew late, and when the day cooled, Julian had a mountain of fine dirt ready to mix with compost, and another huge pile of dry old rocks. Julian had drunk six jars of water.

Juan's boots crunched behind him. Julian was relieved when Juan whistled appreciatively. "You are going to have a difficult time moving tomorrow, amigo. I don't ask that you kill yourself." Juan slapped him on the shoulder. "You better stay home and rest tomorrow, and come back on Wednesday."

"It's no problem, really, *amigo. Por favor,* let me come back tomorrow," Julian said.

"Are you serious?" He shook his head. "No. Trust me. You did too much today. Enough for two days. We'll see you on Wednesday."

The next morning it hurt to move his arms and his back. He felt sick.

"What have you been doing *hijo?*" Marisol asked, sitting down next to him on the rainbow-colored blanket on his bed.

"I'm just getting some work experience, Mama. It's okay. I'm working for Manuel's brother."

"Why, son?"

"I want to do something worthwhile and important, rather than waste my summer, like I did last year. Maybe I'll stay out of trouble and stay in one piece this year," he smiled.

"He wants to take his girlfriend out," Enrique teased.

"You got a problem with that?" Julian asked, giving Enrique a playful sock in the arm.

"Well, all right, but you rest today," Marisol stated firmly to Julian, ignoring their teasing.

"Okay, Mom. Since you insist," Julian answered, suppressing a smile since Juan had already excluded him from working that day anyway.

For several weeks after, Julian worked with Javier's man, putting new trees on the property, building walkways in the garden, and putting in a fountain. He saved his money carefully.

CHAPTER 9 RIDING TOO FAST

Lena and Alan arrived in Puerta Vallarta for one of their frequent visits with their daughter, Audrey. When they walked into the airport from the windy tarmac after the landing, they were suddenly surrounded by four strange men in black suits with earphones. Alan and Lena froze. Alan twisted his mustache and asked, "Is there a problem, Señors?"

"We are here to protect you, Señor, and your lovely wife."

Lena said, "Protect us from what? Who are you?"

"Señor Neri sent us."

"Has something happened to Audrey?"

"No, Señora. We brought a limousine, compliments of Señor Neri, her husband's brother."

Then Alan began laughing.

"What?" Lena asked, annoyed.

"Manuel's brother sent them for us, Len."

Then Audrey and Manuel emerged from the crowd.

Manuel asked, "How do you like this star treatment?"

Lena put her hands on her hips and demanded in mock anger, "Did you two know that Javier was going to do this?"

"Of course!" Audrey laughed.

As the bodyguards escorted Alan and Lena to the limousine, Manuel and Audrey left them to collect the baggage.

Some bystanders asked Audrey, while pointing to her mother and father, "Who are those people?"

Audrey answered, "Oh, that's Lena, a famous movie star in America."

"Oh, yes. We have heard of her!" they said.

This elicited more giggles from Audrey and Manuel.

When they were all in the limousine, Audrey told her parents what an impression they had made. Lena laughed and waved grandly to the crowd that had gathered around them.

A few nights later, Audrey and Manuel were throwing a party at their house for Alan and Lena. Ricky was allowed to invite some friends, so he invited Julian. Audrey called Javier's wife to invite them. She laughed as she added, "By the way, thank your husband for the special reception at the airport."

"He loves to show off," Adelia said offhandedly.

Audrey asked, "Would you two be able to pick up Julian? We invited Marisol and Julian, but Marisol cannot come because Enrique is sick with a cold."

"We'd be happy to."

On the evening of the party, Javier pulled up in his gold Mercedes and honked the horn. Julian kissed his mother good-bye and a Neri bodyguard opened the car door for Julian. Javier stepped on the gas, accelerating around the corners and the Mercedes sped evenly over the rough cobblestones. Through town,

Javier drove furiously through red lights, too close to pedestrians, and Adelia clutched the handle above the door with one hand and the dashboard with another.

"Slow down!" she cried.

"Shut up!" he ordered as he careened around a corner, sending a passerby jumping back and nearly colliding with a honking, oncoming car.

"You've got to slow down. We have got another's son in our car!" she pleaded.

"I told you to shut up!" he yelled, and he slapped her face. Julian sat frozen in his seat. His jaw clenched and he wanted to say something, but he knew it would only bring down anger on him; it wouldn't help the wife. He glanced at the two bodyguards, who stared straight ahead, mouths set in grim lines. When they arrived at Manuel and Audrey's house, Javier got out, slammed the door and charged up the steps without turning around. A bodyguard nodded his head to Julian to get out, and they both got out, leaving the woman with another bodyguard in the car.

The large, yellow house was well lit, and banana trees grew enthusiastically in the garden. The front half of the house was supported by pillars and the front door was at the top of a long, narrow stairway. At the top of those steps, Javier knocked on the carved door.

"Come in, Come in! How are you, brother? And how is Julian today?" Manuel greeted them warmly and showed them in.

"Couldn't your wife come?" Audrey asked.

"She's in the car. She doesn't want to come in. Leave her alone." Javier said.

"Javier, my good man, welcome. What will you have?" Alan called, coming out from the kitchen with a drink in each hand and his big mustache wreathed in a grin and topped with twinkly eyes.

"Scotch on the rocks, Mac. Make it a double!"

While Julian went to Ricky's room and they played with a Gameboy, Lena went outside and tried to convince Javier's wife to come into the house and join the party. She refused. Javier stayed on as late as anyone in spite of her, and got extremely drunk. He turned from the window where he had been looking down on his car, and staggered. He raised his voice so that the seven remaining guests looked up and stared. "I swear I'm going to get rid of those damn, expensive, good for nothing bodyguards! That bitch would be up here where she belongs if those boys weren't sitting with her. I'm tired of having them around my wife and daughter all the time."

Lena pulled Audrey aside and said quietly, "Have Julian stay the night here. Alan and I will convince Javier to go somewhere else for drinks with us, and to let his wife go home."

Later, on Ricky's upper bunk bed where the boys were both sitting, Julian told Ricky about how he liked working for Javier, but that he didn't like the way he was mean to his wife.

Ricky said, "My dad never liked any of his bosses before he owned the lumber business – that's why he works for himself. Besides, Mom doesn't like Dad's brother much either." He swung his legs energetically.

Julian swung his legs too, and gave Ricky a playful kick. Ricky kicked him back. Then Juian laid back and sighed, "I wish my dad was around. You're so lucky to have a mom and a dad, and such nice grandparents. I wish my dad would have thought about being here for me instead of..."

"I know," Ricky said thoughtfully, gazing down at his mother's sewing center, which shared a corner of his room. "He loved you and little Maribel a lot, though. That's what my parents say, and they knew him pretty well 'cause he was my Dad's best worker. He liked your Dad better than he likes my uncle."

Julian looked at Ricky and smiled, impatiently wiping his eyes, then looked toward the knocking sound that was coming from the door.

Manuel opened the door and announced, "Boys, party's over. Julian, you're staying here tonight. Don't worry. We worked it out with your mom and Javier knows. Lie down and go to sleep now."

"Why do we have to? I'm not tired," Ricky said. Yet, sensing the inevitable, Ricky got into lower bunk bed and lay down.

"Thanks boys. Your mom's tired and you know she doesn't rest until you're asleep, Ricky." He turned out the light. *"Buenos noches hombres,"* he said.

Julian was disoriented when he woke up, but he smelled something sweet cooking. Then he remembered where he was, climbed down from the bed, put on his pants, and found the bathroom. It was huge, right in the house, and had a real flushing toilet. While taking care of business, he heard Ricky and his family laughing and talking. Then he padded into a large, yellow and blue, tiled kitchen. Sun poured through the windows, which overlooked the cobbled street. Ricky, Manuel, Alan and Lena were eating banana pancakes that Audrey was frying. They all smiled at him.

Manuel said, *"Buenos Dios.* Are you hungry?" slapped him on the back, and pulled up a chair for him. Right afterwards, there was a scurrying across the tile rooftop. "Did you hear that?" he asked everyone, wide eyed. "It's our hungry roof friend – an iguana who likes my wife's pancakes." He leaned out of the window and threw a pancake up onto the roof.

Alan laughed, "I like it!" He went to the window, climbed onto the windowsill and peered at the roof. "I see him! Here, Ricky, hand me another pancake." He held that out until the iguana took it from his hand. Meanwhile, Lena had been calling him to get down from the window, but with very little conviction. She hadn't had much luck getting Alan to be careful.

Audrey was nonplussed, and continued cooking. She handed an open-mouthed Julian a plate with a stack of pancakes on it. She laughed, "You look like a baby bird. Eat Julian, and get used to the craziness."

Julian watched Ricky spread margarine generously from a tub and pour syrup onto his pancakes, so he tried it too. This new food was delicious, and Julian thought he could eat it every day instead of his mother's tortillas. It was what Manna from Heaven must taste like.

"Would you like some more?" Audrey asked.

He smiled and shook his head no meekly, as he swallowed hungrily.

She made him a couple more, just in case, and put them on his plate, "Well, if you're too full, you don't have to eat these," she explained.

Alan said, "Julian, don't eat them. Save them for me and the iguana!"

Audrey chided, "Dad!"

Alan laughed. Julian checked Ricky's face to see if they were only kidding, then gratefully and hungrily ate the pancakes. He realized that he didn't want to go home and take care of his little brother, and do housework for his mother, or even play video games by himself. He felt envious of Ricky's family, and he felt guilty about it.

Lena said, "Alan and I are going to go look at our little house in Yelapa. It might be in poor condition, but it could be like a little adventure to deserted island for you boys if you would like to come along."

Alan explained to everyone, "We finally got our house back from the damn Mexican government after Salinas De Gotari stole it. It took about a hundred letters, and a good lawyer, but we did it."

Audrey poured more coffee for the grown-ups. "Manuel and I need to make a trip to the resort today. I've got to get those cottages clean and those gardens cleaned up. Everything is a mess right now! Our last guest really trashed the place and our workers just aren't going to take care of everything unless we're there."

Manuel stood up and helped his wife clear the dishes and clean the kitchen, the dishes making a clatter in the sink, "*Sí, suegro,* business is good now. It's actually possible for the first time since '94 to make good money. Get your little house over there set up again."

To his wife he said, while giving Alan a devilish smile, "It's a good idea to let the boys go with them - the old people need the help more than we do!"

Lena cried out, "Manny!"

Audrey laughed and said, "If only they were a help!"

Ricky cupped his hands and told Julian a secret.

Alan leaned over and looked both boys earnestly in the eyes, "We would like it if you boys could come - and your parents need break from you, Ricky."

"I have to be back by Monday to work for Señor Neri," Julian told him.

"No problem," Alan said, "You can take a taxi boat back home Sunday evening."

"We'll go by your house and tell your mom, and you can pick up some things," Lena said.

Later that afternoon, the grandparents and the two boys, climbed into a small boat with a smelly outboard motor, that turned out to be rather loud. They passed coconut trees and forests, and steep hills, on the dark blue, slightly choppy sea. The boat jumped and dipped in a rhythmic pattern.

Ricky told Julian, "You'll love sleeping in the loft. We can see everything on the beach, and they," he jerked his head toward Alan and Lena, "never even come up there! The fishing is great, too. We can fish right off our front porch!"

Alan and Lena overheard Ricky's remark. Lena's eyebrow threatened to raise, but Alan rolled his eyes and grinned. Then she snorted at how their small freedoms gave them so much happiness.

They rounded the bluff and looked over to the left. They were shocked to see that the house was missing two outer walls. They docked and disembarked. Ricky and Julian ran ahead toward it.

"The loft is torn down!" Ricky called back.

"The furniture is gone!" Lena exclaimed when she caught up.

"Not all of it," Ricky said, "There's a hammock, and a bed."

"Christ almighty," Alan swore, "Those damn fools."

He looked around, switching things on and off, turning knobs as he checked the damage to the house, "Hmm. The water and the electricity are off. Let's go see about getting them turned on again."

"The hotel and restaurant owners next door will fix them. Let's go," Lena said.

Ricky called from the hammock, "We'll stay here!"

Julian looked at his feet, embarrassed. He didn't tell his mother what he was going to do; he asked.

"That's fine," Lena called back as she and Alan walked the trail toward the beachside hotel in the intense sunlight.

A few young boys in swimming trunks called out, "¡Hola, Bigotes!"

They clustered around and asked questions. Julian could see a dark brown boy's arms pointing around the bluff and at the house as they talked excitedly.

"C'mon. Let's go to the beach!" Ricky said.

"Qué buena idea," Julian said, falling off of the hammock with a delighted grin.

A breeze stirred the warm air. The small beach filled up with colorfully dressed people. Women in wrapped yellow skirts walked with pink plastic tubs filled with pie on their heads, and young boys walked up and down the beach with Beagle-sized green iguanas on their shoulders. Young girls in braids with blue ribbons carried ropes of strung beads and shells. Further back, were about a hundred tourists sitting in striped blue, white and yellow chairs, at tables with green umbrellas, and under thatched roofs in deep shade. They all seemed to have a huge, dewy drink in a glass shaped like a bell, or in half a coconut.

"Do you want to buy a piece of pie?" a bored-looking brown girl asked.

"Yes," Ricky said. "Do you want one Julian? Two pies."

They kicked off their shoes, and stepped into the water, while taking deep bites into the caramel pecan pies.

They waded through the slightly cool, clear water, watching their brown feet as if through blue-green glass. Julian felt himself absorbing the heat of the sun through his back.

Ricky said at last, "Maybe they wrecked the house after they found out they had to give it back."

Then they heard loud dance music throbbing over on the water. A moment later, a large ferry cast anchor in the middle of the bay.

Brown-skinned people danced on its decks to the music. Laughter carried to the beach. Groups of people began diving off the sides of the boat and swimming for the beach.

"Look! Grandma and grandpa are going back to the house," Ricky said. "Let's get back."

They scrambled up the sandy beach to meet them along the path.

"Are we going to stay here?" Ricky asked, panting a little.

"That depends on whether you boys are willing to rough it a bit, and help put a few things back in their places." Alan said.

"Sure!" the boys said excitedly.

Alan handed them some sheets and towels to carry. "The hotel gave us these to use, and a lantern. They turned on the water for us, but the electricity is down. So, let's set up the house for tonight."

The two boys and Alan took the bed apart and dusted it, shaking the mattress.

"Every time you move something, boys, watch for scorpions. Shake out everything before you put it on, or use, especially in the mornings," Alan said.

"So what happened to the house, grandpa?"

"Have you boys heard of the former President Carlos Salinas de Gortari? He took over our house for his guests and parties. Then there was a rebellion in Chiapas, the PRI's leading presidential candidate was shot, and everyone was upset about the currency devaluation, so he was too busy to come here towards the end. Little by little, tourists took some things, and the locals began to use the house as a fishing hut. It's okay now. We will fix it. No problem," Alan said.

"Say, why don't you boys see if you can borrow a broom, hammer, nails, and a machete from the restaurant? Then we can fix some of these walls and sweep the floors."

"Okay, grandpa."

So they cut some coconut fronds and tied them up to recreate some of the walls in the living rooms, and to patch holes in the main bedroom. Lena swept the floors, made the beds, wiped down the bathroom fixtures, except the shower, which was made of a giant clamshell that the water flowed over. The walls were made of rocks, and didn't need any cleaning.

In the late afternoon, five men scurried across their living room floor like shadows. Alan called out to them, "Hello. How are you this evening? Doing some fishing? Let me know if you catch any big ones!"

The men drew near, smiled and nodded. "*Sí, Señor. Gracias,*" they said and tipped their hats clumsily while they clutched their wooden poles and buckets. After they left, they quickly and quietly scrambled to the outcroppings of rocks beyond the house to fish. For the rest of the trip, the fishermen were careful to use the boulders to climb on, and not the living room floor.

"And now, how about some dinner?" Lena said. She lit a lantern, and they walked the path to the restaurant, stopping on their way to view a pair of scorpions that were mating. At the restaurant, they returned the tools they borrowed and ate some octopus soup with a rich red broth and crispy fried red snapper with onions.

The boys went to bed right after dinner, while Alan and Lena played cards, drank beer, and read.

The next the morning, the boys went fishing and caught a few Roosterfish.

When Lena awoke, she shook out her jeans, and pulled them on, zipping them and snapping the waistband closed. She felt a burning pain near her tailbone, and struggled to get the jeans off. She felt another pain like hot grease on her lower back, "Ouch!" She cried out as she got the jeans unsnapped, "Oh my God! Alan, help!"

Alan told her to lie on her stomach on the bed while he pulled the jeans off. The scorpion crawled out of the jeans, and down the back pocket stitching onto the rocks and escaped outside. The boys heard the commotion and came to see what was the matter, Alan yelled to them, "Get the local herbal doctor!"

Meanwhile, he clambered down the rocks and scooped up some cold wet sand and mud and applied it to Lena's back. She was crying and swearing, "Goddammit, as soon as I feel better, I swear, I'm going to exterminate every crawling thing in that house!"

Alan's face was almost as anguished as hers, "I should have known there would be an accident; the place is infested now."

From the town that looked like pastel candies piled on the hill, an old lady in her black shawl tottered over. She kneeled beside Lena and placed a hand on her trembling shoulder. After raising the small green bottle of the antidote, she measured, and spooned some into Lena's mouth. She washed the wounds, and applied herbal poultices. Alan gave Lena a couple of aspirin and a cup of brandy – his cure for every ailment that anyone had. Later that day, Alan and Lena stayed in two striped chairs on the beach and drank a number of Margaritas. They met with some of the long-term guests, tourists that come once a year for three to six months, and got to talking about Lena's brush with wildlife, and the local herbal expert, who helped her.

"Does the old white doctor still live up the hill over there?" Lena asked.

"Yes, he does. He doesn't do much anymore, of course, but there were a couple of eye infections that he referred to a doctor in town. Real sad thing, too. They both came back missing an eye."

Lena and Alan looked at each other.

"Well, son-of-a-bitch!" Alan said.

CHAPTER 10 THE BODYGUARDS

Javier scowled at Pedro, who was laughing with his beautiful, oldest daughter by the kitchen door. He said to Victor, "I don't need my bodyguards anymore. I especially dislike that Pedro. He's the worst."

Victor, enjoying the shade of Javier's large, newly planted trees said, "They may be expensive, but paying the extra money is better than being robbed, or worse, Javier. Everyone remembers who won the lottery: you haven't let anybody forget it!" he concluded, swirling his vodka on the rocks and nestling deeper into the white wicker chair in Javier's courtyard.

Javier gestured emphatically and declared, "It's a waste of money now. It's been two years – look at that wolf, sniffing around my daughter!" His dark brown forehead wrinkled as he continued to frown at the flirting pair, who were pushing each other playfully.

"Are you going to let him go?"

"I'm going to tell *all* of them *marcharse* – to beat it! Look at them, standing around doing nothing, and I pay them for that!"

Victor peered at the other black-suited guard on the other side of the wrought iron gate, and shook his head, "I'm warning you; it's not safe. You know I don't really read that rag I publish, but it puts me in touch with the fact that this country is full of *pendejos* whose idea of a great way to become a rich man is to kill off one."

Pedro followed the daughter into the kitchen and was chased out with a snapping dishtowel. Javier could hear his daughter laughing and telling Pedro that if he came near again, she'd have *him* play with the baby while *she* stood around and watched.

Javier called, "Guards, get over here!"

Julian stopped his work in the garden, as did the others. They had planted two long rows of trees and were now putting in a cement walkway. The rich smell of earth surrounded him. Julian had been bending form boards and hammering them into place, but he idly held his hammer, while watching the two guards in black suits amble toward Javier.

"Here is your money for this week." Javier counted out stacks of pesos that he had removed from his money belt. Javier's paunch was exposed in a triangle where a corner of his shirt was caught on the belt. He had grown fat since he'd won the lottery two years ago. The stacks of pesos rustled. It took so many pesos to pay for things these days, Javier thought with irritation.

The dark faced senior bodyguard tightened up, instinctively preparing to prevent the loss of a decent job. They were hard to find. He said, "Señor Neri, there is no need to pay us now. Is this stupid buck the cause of the trouble?" He slapped the back of Pedro's head. "You should have told me. Fire him! Señor, you need me. There are many gangs that know of you. I hear things and

I have warned those parasites away. I have protected you and your daughter well."

"You've been helpful. Here is 1800 pesos for you, and you." He counted out money into their open palms.

"Now, adios to you. Your services are no longer needed!"

"You're going to regret this, Señor Neri," the lead bodyguard hissed.

Julian watched the men as they stalked to the gate. Outside the fence, he heard them quarreling, and then they shushed each other.

Early the next morning, at Javier's huge carved door, there was an insistent pounding. The maid roused herself and sleepily opened the door. She should not have opened the door that morning. Three men in ski masks pushed their way into the house. One grabbed the maid, covered her mouth, and pointed a gun at her.

"Take me to Señor Neri," another commanded.

She walked to the door of his room, whispering, "Have mercy. Don't shoot. Please, in the name of Jesus, don't shoot me."

One of them kicked in the Neri's bedroom door.

Adelia sat up in her bed. When she saw the guns, she screamed.

Javier sat up and yelled, "What the hell is the matter?!" He reached for his glasses. When he saw the men clearly, he said, "What do you want? Money?"

"*Sí Señor.* One million dollars."

"I don't have it," he countered.

"Then she will have to get it for you," one said, nodding toward the wife as he pulled Javier to his feet. "You are coming with us for a little visit."

At that moment, the children came to the door of their parent's bedroom.

"Papa, mama!" they cried, as they stood there in their pajamas.

"My children! Let me go to them," Adelia pleaded.

"Go," one signaled for her to go to them.

The men hustled Javier out the front door. He was wearing only his underwear and glasses. His overweight body looked as defenseless as a plucked chicken in the garden's morning sun.

"Open the gate!" one commanded.

The maid scurried to get the key and opened it.

Two men led the nearly-naked Javier to the car while his wife in her nightgown and the younger child watched. The oldest daughter was still pulling on her robe when she came out the door and joined them.

"What's happening, Mama?" she asked quietly.

But before she could answer, a man grabbed the Señora's shoulder, "No police!" he shouted at her. "Do you understand me? You are not to get the police involved, nor should you tell anyone. Get the one million dollars. I will be calling you."

"Yes. I will," she said, pulling away from him.

"If you tell the police, we will kill him," he repeated.

As they got in the black sedan, Adelia followed a short distance away, trying to make a mental note of the license plate number. She ran to the phone, still grateful to have one, even after two years. While she nervously dialed, then waited for an answer, a memory intruded about when the phone was installed. It had cost $2,000 American money – an astounding amount to her. Her husband used to stay busy before he won the Mexican National Lottery, running a fishing business, and they couldn't afford a telephone. *We were safer then*, she thought ruefully, wiping tears from her cheeks. Now here were these men wanting a *million* American dollars from them.

"Hello, could you connect me to the police chief, Armando García? Yes, I'll wait.

"Hello, Armando? *Hola.* I am so glad I could reach you. *Mal, muy mal*, Javier has just been kidnapped."

Chief García smiled, "That's a good one!" he laughed, "Is Manuel putting you up to this little joke? I'm going to give him a traffic ticket just for being on the road next time I see him if he did."

The police chief, Armando García, had recently made a successful campaign in Puerto Vallarta, cleaning the streets of thieves. He was proud of the recent drop in crime, and his bigger police force in the streets. He even provided them with new white

99

outfits, including shorts and safari hats. The tourists not only felt safer, they enjoyed the friendly look of the policemen. So no one could have been kidnapped today.

"No!" Adelia began to sob, "This is not a joke! There were three men wearing masks and they just took him! I got part of their license plate number, 114."

Armando rubbed his forehead and thought, hard. These inside gangster-style jobs were tougher to combat. Javier almost had it coming though. He flaunted his money. He was low class. Nonetheless, he had become an influential person since he won the lottery. He was also a fun drinking buddy.

Armando asked, "Did anyone hurt you? Are your children all right?"

Adelia said, "Sí, I'm fine, and so are they. I'm just worried about my husband. Please don't tell anyone, or make it a police case, officially. I need your help, Armando, as a friend who would know what to do – they will kill him if they find out that the police know!"

"I will pay your home an unofficial visit tonight as a friend only," Armando said.

"You won't wear your uniform will you?" Adelia asked.

"Of course not. Do not worry. They will not kill him. What they want is money. Did they tell you how much they want yet?"

"They want a million dollars! American money! I don't know how to get it." Adelia began sobbing. "Javier never let me have anything to do with the money. He only gave me some shopping money now and then. I don't even know our bank account numbers!"

CHAPTER 11 THE DOCTORS

Julian knocked on the door of María's house.

From inside came the musical tones of "*¿Quién es?*"

"It's Julian,"

"María's not up to seeing visitors just now. I'm very sorry."

"*Está bien.* I want to talk to you. I have money for María's new eyes."

Rosa opened the door.

"You have money? How did you get it, Julian?" She stepped out of the house, so that María wouldn't hear; she had become very sensitive to anyone talking about her.

"I worked for Señor Neri, so María could have new eyes. Please do not refuse this money. People helped me, so I must help, too."

"*Dios Mio,*" she said, crossing herself. "May God bless you, dear child."

"I saved three hundred dollars. That is enough for her operation, isn't it?"

"So much! All by yourself?"

"Señor Neri overpaid me," Julian looked away and fiddled with his wallet.

He looked back at her and said, "I guess it's a good thing, since now he is gone. I would have worked until school started to make sure you had enough, but now, this is all I can give you."

"This is an enormous help, Julian. I can never thank you enough. Has Señor Neri gone on a trip somewhere?"

"We don't know where he is, Señora. He was kidnapped."

"No! You are not serious!" she frowned at Julian to see if he was joking.

"When will we be free from all this evil!?" she demanded at last of the sky above Julian's head. Then she spoke softly to him, "I will pray for his safe return. His kindness to you, and to María must be repaid."

Two days later, María and her mother packed a few belongings and squeezed onto the crowded bus for Guadalajara hospital. Young men were hanging by one hand out of the bus' doors, and a dozen women carrying groceries and bags were standing and struggling to balance their loads. The seats were filled with children and old people. María hung on tightly to her mother. The noise of the bus and the unseen people talking while brushing past, frightened her. Men returning home for lunch after labors in the hot sun, smelled of sweat and dirt. Ashamed of how she must look, she hung her head, letting her black, wavy hair hang into her face. A man pinched her from behind, but she just kept her head down. Only her mother's comforting smell and sturdy waist that she held onto like a rosary when she said her prayers, kept her from panic.

Many hours later, they arrived at the hospital and there they had to wait for a long time in a bare room filled with cheap plastic chairs. At last, a nurse called, "Dr. Suarez will see you now."

María walked, guided by her mother's arm around her waist, holding her mother's fringed, red shawl for security.

The doctor's office had a shelf containing supplies, a table and a firm bed. They sat on the bed. Rosa saw a poster showing a huge eye and its parts on one of the walls. She looked away from it.

A young doctor entered. "¿*Qué es esto?*" He looked at María and noted, "A double eye extraction. Hmm." He studied the records in his hands.

"There seems to be no record of this eye extraction. Where was it done?"

"It was done here, doctor. I mean it was this hospital – but the doctor, told me to – We came after the office was closed."

"¿*Como?*" The doctor raised his eyebrows in surprise.

Rosa was afraid she would be punished. Going to the doctor's office after hours was wrong, perhaps. But like a bribe, it was seemingly the only way for a poor person to manage.

An alarming thought occurred to Rosa, This doctor might turn us in to the Ministry of Health! We might not get anything! She glanced at the door.

The doctor asked, "Who performed the surgery?"

"I don't remember."

"Well, where was it done?

Rosa shrugged and watched the door. Now she wished she had waited for Dr. Bella, who would return from Puerto Vallarta in a few days anyway.

The doctor cleared his throat, "I can see that you don't want to talk about this," he said kindly, "but I have an offer that I know you will be interested in. Free prosthetic eyes. The government provides them. Also I have a list of services which can help María to complete some schooling, or learn a profession."

Rosa stood up and shook her head, "*¡Es imposible!* La doctora Bella told me that it would cost me three hundred American dollars!"

His thick brows jammed together and his tender mouth hardened. "Dr. Bella?! Why?" He exhaled and pushed a lock of black hair of his forehead.

Rosa and her daughter were edging toward the door as if to escape. Dr. Suarez suddenly realized he had to calm her down quickly, or they would leave and receive no help at all. He reached over and touched her arm, "*Está bien. No te preocupes.* Don't worry now. You haven't done anything wrong. I am only upset that Dr. Bella told you that the eyes would cost so much. She has made some kind of mistake."

Rosa's loosened her hold on her daughter a little. She hesitated as she examined the doctor's face, "You're serious?"

Dr. Suarez nodded, smiling. "*Sí,* of course." He also told her about special teachers who could assist María with becoming independent and capable. Then he spoke reassuringly to María, as he measured, and checked the health of her eye sockets.

María spoke up, "*Por favor,* could you give them to me now?" Her tear glands were intact, and now tears dripped down her cheeks.

Dr. Suarez had only recently completed his internship, so he hesitated, then nodded his head solemnly. He told a nurse the size and color of the prosthetics she should bring.

After Rosa thanked him and departed with María, he wondered what else he could do. He resolved to report the situation that María and Rosa had described about their experiences with Dr. Bella to the ministry of health. His accounts of Dr. Bella's suspicious activities were listed and filed by a clerk. Then the reports were forgotten.

CHAPTER 12
LOCATING THE RANSOM MONEY

Julian had a few more days to kill before summer vacation ended, so he decided to go to Javier's house to find out if he was back.

Adelia came to the door after the maid told her it was Julian. She was wearing a black and tan tailored dress, finer even than his mother's best church dress. "How are you, Julian? Come in," she said. She told the maid who had paused to get a look at the handsome boy, " Bring him some cold Horchata."

"Are you all well?" Julian asked as he entered. "How is Señor Neri?"

"They let him call me. He says he is fine. He hasn't come home yet, Julian."

"I'm sorry. Can I help you, Señora?"

"There isn't any work right now."

Adelia watched Julian nod sympathetically, and wondered if he could be useful after all. He was a very polite boy, and practically a relative. Then Adelia remembered that she needed help finding Javier's papers in order to locate the ransom money. Last night the raspy, cruel sounding kidnappers had called her – not only to allow her to talk with her husband so that she would know he was alive, but also to wrangle her about locating more money. She sighed.

"Are you feeling all right, Señora Neri?"

"I'm just tired. I stayed up late last night, trying to buy more time from those devils that have my husband. He did all of the banking, so it's hard to get the ransom money."

She did not tell anyone that it was only because the police chief vouched for her that the bank released $100,000 dollars to her.

Remembering how they had threatened to go to her house and "help" her locate more money, she walked over to the sliding glass door and stared out the window at the trees. Julian followed her.

Adelia sighed and said, "My husband has a safe in his office, but I can't even find it!"

"Let me help you!" he said earnestly. "I'm good at gadgets and things, and I've already finished two years of secondary school."

"Yes, you could help me!" she said, turning to face him. "I need to find business papers that belong to Javier, so that I can get the kidnappers to release him. Last night he told me that he had a safe hidden in his office and the combination. The safe is hidden behind some wall plaster."

"I would be honored to help," Julian said in a formal voice he normally reserved for his teachers. He stood up as straight as he could to show that he was the size of a grown man. She smiled wistfully and began to walk to her husband's office. Her heeled shoes clicked along the ornate, hand-painted tiles. Julian followed her down the hallway and marveled at the profusion of furniture in the house. What use could all of these tables, chairs, shelves, mirrors, and trunks have for a small family of four?

At the end of the hall, Señora Neri stopped and explained, "You have to take out a closet wall with a hammer, and open the safe. Javier gave me the combination to the safe – it looks complicated. There is the key that you must turn as well, at the same time, or afterwards or something. Maybe you can make sense of these directions." She walked into the office and there was a hammer, and the key on a desk of carved, dark red rosewood. She nodded toward them. She slid a desk drawer open, retrieved some slips of paper with scrawled notes, and laid them on the edge of the desk.

"Here is the combination." She straightened up and smoothed her black, well-coifed hair.

Julian said softly, "I will try, Señora."

"Don't tell anyone about this, okay?"

Julian stared at her briefly. "Um, okay," he said.

The wall in the closet was battered and dented where Adelia had tried to knock it out. The lock on the safe should be easy – she'd given him the combination and key, and the directions looked like a simple math problem.

He swung the hammer with his strong right arm while she watched. The wall caved in a little. Plaster chunks soon began to fall into the wall space, but inside, the wall seemed as empty as any other. When the hole was as big as a TV screen, he at last hit metal with a resounding thud. By this time, Julian was breathing hard. He kept hitting the wall and the safe. Meanwhile, he worried that he'd hit and break the dials on the face of the safe that he would need to have functioning. He began pulling off chunks of plaster with his hands and revealed the entire front of the safe.

Meanwhile, Adelia plucked bits of skin off of her cuticles until they bled as she watched him make calculated turns to the right and left, in between reading and rereading the instructions while listening for a few telltale clicks. Julian tried the key then and the safe did not open. He scratched his eyebrows and rubbed the sweat off his fuzzy upper lip. He tried using the key first, and then he tried to do both at the same time.

Adelia surmised that it was embarrassing him to have her watch him fail, so she softly stepped out of the room. In fact, Julian had been barely aware of her presence. The task was everything to him at the moment. Julian tried pulling some of the levers on the front of the safe at various times during the process of turning the lock and the key. Within a couple minutes, Adelia called through the door to ask how he was doing and if he needed anything. He didn't, so she left again.

The safe swung open at last to reveal a gun, stacks of papers, money, and some boxes. Julian picked up the black gun and felt its compact, heavy weight, and its coolness. It gave him a sense of nonchalance, self-assurance, and security. He wondered if there were bullets in it. He reached into the safe, and picked up one of the small boxes. It was heavy. Inside, there were neatly ordered silver-colored bullets with shiny brass tops.

It would sure be fun to fire this, he thought. He heard a muffled sound in the house and remembered Adelia would be coming soon. He put the gun in his pants and the bullets in his pocket, untucking his shirt to cover any bulges. Next, he took out the papers, envelopes and money, and put them on the desk. He rubbed his face and forced himself to exhale – he had been holding his breath.

Adelia knocked lightly, "Did you open it, *muchacho*?"

"*Sí*, I think it's what you were looking for, Señora Neri!"

She entered, took the soft seat in front of the desk, and counted the pesos, about $15,000 worth. Then she viewed the lists of investments and property and was relieved. She looked at the light pink and tan papers with their official seals describing the money they had, but realized with despair that it was going to be complicated to release these funds to free her husband.

"I've got to call Manuel for help with these papers." She turned to Julian and smiled, "You've been a wonderful help. *Gracias*." She then showed him to the door. She disappeared for a moment, and returned with ten dollars worth of pesos from the safe.

Julian grinned as he loped down the cobblestone lane, passing verdant terraces, feeling the weight of the gun and bullets against his loins. He had some spending money; and – for all he knew – he had solved Adelia's problems. Javier might be free soon. María was probably getting her new eyes and would begin talking to her friends again. Julian had a gun and could end his life, but now he wanted to live.

A gun could be put to better use, he thought.

CHAPTER 13 THE BARGAIN

Adelia turned to the telephone after she closed the door and called Manuel. "I need your help to turn these papers that I have found into cash. They threatened to come for my daughter too, if I don't hurry!"

Manuel and Audrey came over to Adelia's house that evening. When they were seated in the dining room near tall, open windows, thunder growled within the black clouds behind the lace draperies. Lightening flashed, rain began falling, and water splashed in over the sills and onto the hardwood floor. Adelia closed the casements, yet the rain and thunder could still be heard. Various intensities of flashes would continue to punctuate their conversation.

When they were resettled, Manuel asked Adelia, "Did you call a reporter and tell them about Javier's kidnapping?"

"No, of course not! I didn't even tell the police!"

"Well, there is a big story in the paper, and it has a *lot* of detail. Was my brother really kidnapped in his underwear?"

Adelia's face darkened with embarrassment, "Yes, it is true! But the only person I told was the police chief, as a friend. He swore not to tell anyone! Why would he tell people?" she asked them forlornly.

Everyone looked at each other, as if one of them might know the answer.

After a pause, Adelia asked with clenched fists, "Did Victor print it?"

Audrey shook her head, "No. It was that other paper."

Manuel questioned Adelia, "Did you recognize any of them? Did any of them sound like the bodyguards that Javier had fired?"

"I don't know. I saw part of the license plate of the car that they drove away in, and I told the police chief. He hasn't told me any news since then, though."

Manuel absently rubbed the sparse black hairs on his dark muscular legs below his shorts, "I wonder why the police chief hasn't said anything about the license plate numbers. Is it just that they are that slow and disorganized?"

"It probably is, honey," Audrey said.

"*Sí, es posible,*" Manuel agreed. Then he demanded, "Why would he leak information to the press, if he did? He's been trying to clean up crime and preserve the image of safety, so the tourists will keep coming here."

"Maybe the kidnappers leaked the information to the press," Audrey said.

Adelia cried, "But the kidnappers said they would kill him if we told anybody! Also, the truth is, I'm willing to give them the money, but I don't know how!"

"Let me see the papers you found," Manuel said gently.

Adelia got up, left the room, and returned with the messy sheaf of papers that Julian had gotten out of the safe from the office. Manuel spread them out on the lace covered, carved, walnut table that the three of them were seated around in the spacious dining room.

"The boat can be sold easily," he said, watching her reaction. She nodded, keeping her eyes lowered.

"These American stocks can be sold easily as well. As a matter of fact, some of these stocks should bring in a very large sum. He must have gotten some good advice somewhere."

"Maybe Victor helped him," Audrey said.

A warm rain began coming down so hard, that Manuel checked the ceiling and looked outside.

Suddenly, Manuel realized that Victor, with his connections to U.S. businesses and Mexican organized crime, could indeed help them. In fact, he may know quite a bit. Then Manuel wondered if Victor had set Javier up. In any case, it would be a good idea to enlist Victor's help, and then watch him closely.

Manuel located one hundred and forty thousand dollars within the next two days. During this time, the kidnappers had taken to calling Adelia nightly and badgering her about the money. Adelia was afraid to talk to the kidnappers again, and Audrey volunteered to stay with her for a couple nights. She would coach Adelia on what to say, or take the phone if necessary.

Manuel became irritated with his brother once again, for being a difficult, irascible, and stubborn man. He would throw his money away to make a big impression on others, but when it came to saving his own skin, he wasn't being very helpful.

Manuel wasn't happy about Audrey spending the night there either, but he smiled with pride at her goodness and spunk. That was why he had married her, an American woman - and he had prospered with her father's help.

Becoming very concerned about Audrey's safety on the third night, he decided to stay over as well. Manuel called the maid at home. She agreed to stay in the house and watch over Ricky. Then Audrey talked with Ricky on the phone, and he said he was fine. He would watch another couple of American videos.

At 9:30 the kidnappers called. Adelia answered the phone, "*Hola. ¿Quién habla? Sí*, I can prove to you that I am getting the money. I have $215,000 ready for you right now."

"We know you have millions, you whore! You can get more money than that. We will only continue to treat your husband decently as long as you keep finding more money."

"*Uno momento, por favor*, I spilled hot soup on my dress," Adelia said, she covered the phone and relayed the conversation to Audrey rapidly.

"Tell him he'll have his money, soon, but large funds like he is asking for take time to gather. Tell him that anyone familiar with money at all would understand that."

The insulting tone of the message worried Adelia and she hesitated, but Audrey signaled to go ahead.

Upon hearing this message, the kidnapper hesitated.

Sensing her advantage, Adelia asked, "May I speak to my husband please?"

There were muffled sounds through the phone, and a minute wait, then, "Adelia? *Sí, estoy bien.* They gave me a very good dinner. I have warm clothes."

Adelia heard several men speaking angrily in the background, then a rough voice spoke into the phone, "Señora Neri, you were very foolish to inform the press. It may be easier for us to kill him and bury him in the desert than to keep waiting for such a worthless woman. Send whatever you have to the Chiapas post office, to "Don Juan." If you don't, your husband will be rotting under the hot sand."

That night, Audrey put a hysterically crying Adelia to bed with a whiskey and warm milk.

In the morning, Manuel volunteered to deliver $200,000 American money to the kidnappers himself. He told Adelia, who was relieved.

117

However, later, when he told his wife, she shouted at him, "You can't do that. It's stupid! They might just shoot you and take the money! Hire someone else to do it!"

"If I hire some guy and he gets killed, what then? I will be responsible for his death."

"I don't care! The person who is hired will choose to take that risk, not you. What about Ricky and me? Don't you care about us, or just your creepy brother?"

"That's not fair. Of course I care about you and Ricky more than anything. You wouldn't understand. This is something that I have to do myself."

"Oh! You macho idiots! This whole country is full of fools!" Audrey cried. Then she stormed out of the Neri's home.

Adelia stared wordlessly at Manuel.

He said, "Don't worry. She'll get over it. I'll get him back. Give me the money."

At home, Audrey refused to speak to Manuel. She even packed up Ricky and took him to the resort with her. She spent most of the next day talking long distance with her mother and father in the United States on the phone about her stubborn husband and her fears for him. When she wasn't doing that, she was working viciously to eradicate dirt and weeds from the grounds – and anger from her heart.

In the morning, Manuel drove their van, carrying the American cash, out to a lonely area surrounded by trees, where a small gas station, a post office, and a few crumbling adobe and tile buildings stood. He got out and walked around a little, but stayed near his van.

A dilapidated, loud, VW pulled up. The man inside wore a bandanna over his mouth, a straw hat, and sunglasses, "Are you looking for the post office?"

"Yeah."

The man scanned the surroundings, "You here solo?"

"Yep."

"Do you have money for Don Juan?"

"Are you one of the kidnappers?"

"No, they just hired me – hurry up!"

Manuel reached for the front passenger seat and brought out a tan mailing envelope, bulging in the middle. He held it up for the other man to see, stepped forward, and handed it to the man. The man looked inside, nodded, and said, "You tell Señora Neri that she will get a phone call in one more week, at night. She better have more by then, and be ready to deliver it."

Once he was back at home, Manuel called Mr. Todd for advice.

Mr. Todd said, "If I were you, I'd call that newspaper guy, Javier's friend. See if he knows about his buddy's investments. I

119

bet they talk about their money with each other plenty. Victor sounds like a street-smart guy. Maybe he'll level with you."

Right after he hung up, Manuel called Victor at his office for any information he might have about Javier's stocks. Victor knew about some of Javier's investments, and locating more money became a bit easier. They agreed to meet at the Neri home. Victor drove to Javier's house. When he arrived, it was lunch time. Adelia scurried about in her pink, polka dot dress, seeing to it that her maid served a fine meal to her guests: Carne Asada, and tender beef tongue in green chile, served with corn tortillas and melons. Adelia had even put pink and white carnations on the table. It made her feel better.

After lunch, she, Manuel, and Victor took his limousine downtown. They got out in the business section near the government buildings. They walked between the manicured lawns and fountains that divided the busy streets. Manuel and Adelia followed Victor through a large brass door into a spacious, marble building with brass trim and glass dividers between the front offices for the paper. The printing was done in the dirty area in the back of the building.

Javier's stock portfolio was more accessible now, since Victor was deferred to as a powerful trader. Adelia, with the police chief's confidential letter verifying what had happened to Javier – as if the whole town didn't already know – was able to get herself a lawyer.

Afterwards, she and Victor got a special, temporary, power of attorney. Also right there in his office, Victor used his computer to open The Bank of the Future, Mexican stocks traded abroad, called the ADR's, on the Internet.

Victor told them not to worry, "Those amateurs have nothing to gain by killing him," he said, "They need to move on now that the story is in the news. Even the thieves we call the police might find those kidnappers! It is the bodyguards he fired that did this - thrown off the job with no notice – they won't find paying customers for weeks or months, maybe."

He snorted, "That blockhead never did treat them with diplomacy. I'm sorry, Señora Neri." He glanced at her apologetically, and then said,

"Adelia, offer them the other $200,000 after we sell the boat. That's $400,000. They will take it and leave. *¿De Acuerdo?*"

Adelia looked to Manuel.

"How can you be so sure?" Manuel asked.

Victor leaned back and smelled the deep scent of his leather chair, "Those guys aren't killers. They were angry and broke. They knew Javier was no longer protected. Besides, Javier will never be able to prove it was them if they leave. $400,000 could take them and their families to the Los Estados Unidos, Costa Rica, or any number of places. The police won't chase them," He laughed, "Ha! They can barely afford gas for their cars, unless they take bribes."

Adelia clutched her black, patent leather purse tightly. She had to sell the boat; the one place where she and her husband had still frequently had romantic times before he was kidnapped. "I can't thank either of you enough," she said.

"I'm afraid it's not quite over yet, but you are quite welcome. I'll have you taken home," he called his chauffeur.

After Adelia was gone, Victor leaned forward and opened a wooden humidor with brass edging and a dial on the inside displaying the humidity readings. He pulled out a fat cigar. "Would you like a cigar? They're the good Cuban ones."

"Yes, I would," Manuel said with a look of amusement. Victor lit it for him. After a luxurious puff, he rubbed the stubble that was forming on his dark brown face, and fixed his eyes on Victor's expectantly.

Victor crossed his feet on the table near the humidor, "So, now that you know where the big boys trade, would you like to join? I can show you where to put your money to work."

"I'm more interested in your knowledge of the criminal sector, Victor."

Victor's eyes suddenly narrowed, yet he smiled politely, "Why, what tickles your curiosity, Manuel? What would you like: girls, drugs, imports, or maybe a foreign bank account?"

Manuel laughed, and then waived those ideas away with a motion of his hands while he took a puff on the cigar. He exhaled and said, "Have you heard anything about the eye specialist that works here and in Guadalajara?"

Victor raised his eyebrows and asked skeptically, "Oh, you need a transplant for your eye?"

"I know a young girl who does."

"Does she have money?"

"That can be arranged."

Victor leaned forward conspiratorially, " Your mistress has glaucoma?"

Manuel was taken aback, but chuckled and said, "No, it's a young girl that is a friend of my son's." Then he relayed the situation about María and Julian, leaving nothing out.

Victor frowned and said, "That doctor is getting money from someplace she shouldn't, and it won't be hard to find out where. I can have my reporters check all her business accounts. I'll check her phone records. I have friends at TELMEX."

Manuel felt relieved. He was anxious that the lady who almost blinded Julian would be brought to justice.

Adelia played with her children the following week, trying to be cheerful, as she awaited the call from the kidnappers. The low point of the week was when she had to hand the title of the boat over at the docks, the boat she and her husband had taken Victor, his girlfriend, a bodyguard, and Julian on a fishing trip not long ago.

Two male buyers –Victor was sure they were drug runners – roughly handed her wads of cash, which was all she would take, since cash was what the kidnappers wanted. She had teetered on the docks in her heels, frowning as she tried to count the money in the slight breeze. Victor had stood by watching the men closely, and eyeing the boat mournfully.

As soon as the transaction was complete, Victor breathed in deeply of the sea air and smiled at Adelia. He knew that she had enough money for another boat, and plenty besides, but kept this to himself for now, lest she try to give it all to the worthless kidnappers. In his opinion, Adelia was too fine a woman for Javier, finer than any he had been able to find yet.

Victor's ability to garner large bribes from officials for falsified and skewed newspaper stories made him one that few would cross. He had bought a newspaper business with money from illegal imports, so he loved a good deal and didn't mind bending the truth.

When the call came, Manuel and Victor were assembled in the Neris' spacious living room. Audrey had stayed home at Manuel's insistence – which did nothing to ease the tension between them.

Victor turned off the large color TV. Adelia answered with panache. She had been coached by each of them.

"Yes, but all I could come up with is $200,000 more. You don't understand how difficult it is to liquidate investments! You don't seem to realize that our money is elsewhere!"

There was a long pause. Adelia looked questioningly at her comforters. Her eyes were round with fear.

Victor made an obscene gesture to suggest that the kidnappers were "whacking off" in order to kill time. He was confident that the kidnappers had reached their limit. Manuel, in spite of being nervous on behalf of his brother, felt the edges of his mouth twitch with amusement, and a little of Victor's assurance seeped in.

"We will meet you with the money. What? At the docks?"

Victor shook his head no.

"Um, no. I was too sad to have to sell the boat; I don't want to see the docks. Would the plaza be okay?"

Another long pause. Manuel smiled at Adelia. She wasn't such a simpleton after all. All she needed was a little education.

"No. By the stage. Tonight?" Adelia looked at her companions for direction. Manuel and Victor exchanged glances and nodded in the affirmative.

"Okay. When? In half an hour?" She glanced at Victor, who agreed.

Soon after, Victor and Manuel walked to the dark, deserted amphitheater. Manuel noticed a few lovers strolling along the sidewalks in the plaza, and along the beach where the waves lapped softly. Across the street, the bars were quiet except for soft guitar music, faintly audible in the breeze. Silhouettes of empty, canvas booths lined the plaza where earlier there had been jewelry sellers and tamale stands. Palm trees were silver-lined in the moonlight.

What lovely surroundings in which to buy back his own brother! Since conversing with his American father-in-law, Manuel had become slightly more impatient with corruption. But, like body odor in the warm months, you take the bad with the good.

They waited for almost an hour. Were they too late, or were the kidnappers late? Manuel wondered, his stomach contracting. Then, a black sedan pulled up near the stage area fifteen feet away. Out came three men. Victor and Manuel stood together near the wooden stage.

Two men, hats pulled down, with hands in their pockets, stood near the car. The white-haired man wore dark glasses and held a handkerchief to his nose as if he had a bad cold. He gruffly asked if they had the money. Victor hefted it onto the stage, and the man opened the case and counted carefully.

"Where is Javier?" Manuel said.

"He's in the car," the man answered without looking up from the money.

"When will you let him go?"

"We will drop him off at his house," the man said. "There had better be no police."

Then he turned and walked away with the payment.

At her home later, that night, Adelia heard the scuffling and pounding at the gate. She impulsively opened the door, and there was Javier, wearing only his underwear and glasses.

"Hi." He said in a hoarse voice.

Adelia began laughing, and said, "Ay, you're safe. Come in."

She shut the door and hugged him. "You've lost weight!" she exclaimed.

Javier smiled weakly. "I can't say the same for you."

"I look just fine!" Adelia said.

"You certainly do." He kissed her, and said, "I need a drink. A strong one!"

CHAPTER 14 THE GUN

Ricky, thin, but gaining muscle and form in his arms, held up the slightly battered mannequin's head that he had found behind the pink, cement walls of Audrey's store. He said, "This is so perfect for target practice! This will be great, no?"

Julian was trying to release the safety on the gun. He was sweating with nervousness, but he had the good sense to keep the gun pointed away from Ricky. "*¿Sí, como no?* Put the victim over there," he pointed to a decrepit fence under an avocado tree.

The dry, tall grass brushed against Ricky's jeans as he searched for a tall stick to impale the head upon. Julian's senses seemed heightened. He double-checked to see that no one was about. It was quiet, siesta time, and very hot. There were few houses within range. The mile-wide yards and empty lots provided the perfect place to try out his aim with the stolen gun.

His hand trembled slightly and he cursed. Beads of perspiration dripped into his eyes. As he wiped his forehead, he looked around for Señor Neri, but reminded himself that Neri was a penned pig. "*Está bueno,*" he called to Ricky, who had set up the grotesquely out-of-place female head.

Ricky strode back to where Julian stood, and waited behind Julian, "*¿Estás listo?*"

"*Sí,*" Julian raised the gun with one hand, having only seen guns fired in movies, peered along the black sights, repositioning until he could make out the blurry, peach-colored blob that was the mannequin head. He pulled back the trigger slowly. With a loud explosion the gun recoiled, throwing him off balance. He caught himself by stepping back several times.

Ricky whooped, "¡*Ay, caramba!* Let's see what you hit!"

The boys ran over to the head and looked for the bullet. They couldn't find it.

"Try again! You must have missed."

This time Julian held the gun with two hands, arms straight out. Again he aimed, pressed the trigger slowly, until the gun fired. When the kickback pushed him, his strong brown legs staggered less. The boys looked at each other wordlessly, then both ran to the mannequin again to see. This time, there was a bullet lodged deep inside the head. Julian pulled the bullet out of the foam. He said, "Look! The bullet is so small now!"

"Is that little thing really big enough to hurt a bad guy?'

"*No sé.* It must be," Julian studied the gun in his hands with renewed appreciation, "Here, you try it."

"This is going to be great!" Ricky cried as he began to run with the gun in his hand.

Julian hurried after him, calling, "¡*Cuidado!* Be careful."

Ricky held the gun with two hands, for he had been watching Julian. He raised the gun, and Julian noticed that Ricky didn't steady the gun long enough to sight the target. Ricky fired the gun and lost his balance.

"¡*Cabrón!* She pushes hard!" Ricky laughed.

"You didn't even look for the target, *tonto*," Julian said playfully.

"Well, let's go see."

The bullet was nowhere to be found, so they practiced some more, taking turns, teasing. Julian struggled with reloading the gun, truly frightened, breathing short shallow breaths. He removed the magazine from the handle, and correctly placed the bullets inside, the points facing the tip of the barrel. He pushed the magazine back in. When he attempted to fire the next time, the bullets jammed.

Ricky said, "*Pues*, let's go. That's enough for today. Someone might come."

"I've got to get this right," Julian said, his face tense, lips tight with determination.

"Are you planning to shoot somebody?"

"I just want to know how this works, that's all. Why don't you go home?" Julian paused, "I'll see you later."

Ricky stayed, and he just watched Julian. Julian kept working with it until the action moved smoothly, while Ricky threw rocks. When Julian was satisfied, he fired off one more shot then went to collect the head, "Do you want to keep this?" he called.

"*¿Estás loco?* My mother would get sick with worry!"

Back at home, Julian watched his brother build a truck with old Tinker Toys. Then he played with Enrigue by making a balding GI Joe doll talk about the truck and the adventures he had with it. There was a soft knock at their front door. Julian opened the door slowly.

His voice cracked. "¿Señora Neri, *como está?*" He forced a polite smile. Her nose looked swollen, and one eye seemed to have dark circles or dark blue makeup smeared on it. His stomach sank and his limbs became loose. *Maybe the kidnappers beat her up*, he thought.

"Who hurt you, Señora?"

"I'm just clumsy. It doesn't really hurt." She touched her face lightly. "But there is something you can help me with muchacho. *Es muy importante*, Julian. Did you take anything from the safe before you gave me the papers?"

His lips were dry and he had to go to the bathroom. Should he tell her? Was this his chance to come clean and be forgiven? He couldn't look at her as he lied.

"No."

"Did you see a gun in the safe?"

"No," he lied again. "Why do you ask me?"

"I didn't close the safe after you left, afraid I wouldn't be able to open it again. I didn't know that we had a gun, but my husband

131

is—upset. He says that his gun is missing. I must help him find it. Well, I'm sorry to bother you."

Julian said good-bye and closed the door. He leaned against it and closed his eyes, feeling terribly guilty. *So many people have helped me, so why am I doing this?*

"Bang!" you're dead!" his little brother shouted. "I shot you, so you have to fall!"

Startled, Julian's eyes flew open.

Enrique was pointing his GI Joe's arm at him, and sighting through the doll's imaginary gun.

"Don't be so violent!" Julian scolded, and he slumped onto the bed next to his brother. He rationalized his choice. Señor Neri could easily get another gun, and he couldn't. He needed it to avenge himself and María.

CHAPTER 15 THE CUSTOMER

An American, named Nadia, wore large prescription sunglasses and a wide-brimmed hat to protect her face from wrinkles – better late than never. From a distance, she looked strikingly sexy. She strode, as huffily as possible in heels and a bikini, up to the edge of a pool. She called out to a blond man who was sitting at the in-pool bar in one of Monterrey's deluxe hotels. After she took off her heels, the man helped her into the pool, and led her to a stool next to him.

"Thanks, Honey," She said. "I'm so mad! The eye bank in Monterrey has a waiting list that's no better than the eye banks in the states!"

David cursed. "Well, screw them! There are more eye doctors in Mexico. Let's head to Guadalajara. What the hell?"

Momentarily soothed, she kissed his naked shoulder, cocked her head and observed his submerged, slender hips. Then the shimmering of the pool blurred her vision, like fish scales on her eyes.

David pensively took a sip of his Corona. If Nadia needed an cataract surgery, or whatever, he figured he could help her get it. If they went to a large city and made appointments with the eye doctors there, they might find someone who could manage it without the eye banks....

He studied everything and almost anything in his ample spare time, for he was curious, but easily bored. So what if Nadia was fifteen years older than he? She looked pretty damn decent to him.

Nadia ordered a Piña Colada and languidly settled on a submerged barstool next to him. David admired her tanned ample breasts pushing up out of a white bikini top. She rubbed the rim of her glass as she set it on the bar, "I wonder if the religious fervor of these people prevents them from donating body parts after someone dies?"

He shook his head, "Nah. These people would probably sell their own mother if they could buy a better life with some American bucks."

Nadia continued, "But people waste so many useful parts just because they are afraid to show up in heaven with missing eyes and hearts." She lit a cigarette. "You're right though. Some of these people could sure use some money. It's a shame that we're not allowed to just pay people to donate good eyes and other parts from their dearly departed."

"Well, you know things work differently here, sweetie. It's just who you pay that matters," David stole a puff from her cigarette. "I read the other day that it doesn't even change the way the dead person looks when they remove the eyes. Only a thin layer of the eye comes off for a cornea, but if they take the whole eye, maybe they put glass ones in or something. That way, if you have an open casket burial, the dead person doesn't look bad. The Catholics here like open casket burials, so that's a good thing to mention, if we get a seller."

"Is there nothing you won't read about? What a terrible thought!" She reconsidered after a moment, "Still, that is an interesting point.... You really are a self-taught intellectual!" She stroked his hair, and he rubbed her back absently while he sipped his beer. Then he lit himself a cigarette, since hers was gone.

David drove Nadia in her silver Lexus to Guadalajara. They checked into La Tapatía, another fine hotel with an in-pool bar, this one with a colonial look. The next day, they walked to the hospital to find an eye specialist. They linked arms, and he helped her navigate, safely crossing the streets during breaks in the speeding traffic.

When they arrived at the dilapidated, sandstone hospital, they were surprised how crowded the lobby was. At last they got to speak to a nurse, and Nadia explained that she needed a good eye surgeon.

The nurse said, "La doctora Bella is the most famous in the whole city."

"Then she is the doctor I absolutely must have!" Nadia gushed. "When can I see her?"

The nurse said, "The next patient is already late, so we can fit you in." She read Nadia's age as she picked up the medical information sheet, "*¡Qué bella eres!* How have you stayed so young and beautiful?"

"It's taken a lot of work, honey," Nadia assured her, the gold bracelets on her wrist glinting as she waved her hands.

The nurse made an almost imperceptible curtsey. She understood not what Nadia had said, but the wealth that Nadia exuded, and rushed to get her seen. In this way, she might in turn please Dr. Bella, who was difficult and taciturn toward most hospital workers. She led Nadia to a plain-looking room that didn't smell as clean as the rooms in Monterrey, or in America. The uncovered, gray trash can was full.

Dr. Bella entered the room wearing her shiny stethoscope and white lab coat. Nadia smiled obsequiously.

Dr. Bella asked, "So, have you been examined by an American doctor?"

"Yes, but I can't get the recommended treatment; a corneal transplant."

Dr. Bella raised one eyebrow skeptically, "Why not? Is it too expensive?"

"No," Nadia hesitated, "It's because I smoke and drink. The damn American doctors want to give the donations to the most saintly people first. They say I have to go without drinking for a year, because I had a…" Nadia sensed somehow that she had better be straight forward with this doctor, even though she had lied about this over at The Eye Bank in Monterrey, "a DUI, a drunk driving record."

Dr. Bella listened to Nadia's story with her head cocked to one side, and her eyes narrowed. To her, it sounded like a lie that police would make such a big deal out of drinking and driving, since that was normal. Nor could she believe that doctors and police had any contact, since that never happened.

Nadia began to gesture wildly as she spoke, "So the transplants keep going to other people first. I don't know what they want in Monterrey! Maybe a person who can give them a political gift, or government grants. Or maybe they don't want to give out anything to an American!"

Dr. Bella's voice had a hard, sharp edge, "What makes you think *I* can provide a transplant, if they can't?"

"I don't know! All I know is I need it! I'm going blind, and if you would at least look at my eyes, you would see that. The only reason I came here is because I haven't looked here yet. I've looked all over the United States, and I've already looked in Monterrey. I heard that sometimes a person dies and the family donates the eyes to the local hospital."

"Hmm, yes, that's true sometimes. You really want this, don't you?"

Nadia sniffled and nodded, wiping a tear.

"Well, I'll see what I can do. Look into this light, straight ahead."

The damage that Dr. Bella saw within Nadia's eyes was enough to render a person blind. It would be as if one were trying to look through a waterfall.

Dr. Bella might have become a compassionate and caring person, if she had not had to fight to survive. Education was expensive. Many girls she knew became prostitutes, and others became slaves to passels of children and their no-good, drunken, cheating husbands. She wanted independence above all.

For remaining single, she had been mistrusted. In addition, she was paid lower wages than male doctors. As a result, she despised most men, and gathered as much money, the stuff of survival, as she could.

"You know," Dr. Bella said, while squeezing dilation inducing drops into Nadia's eyes with her manicured fingers, "it will take some time and a lot of money to get a transplant. Many families of the recently departed are reluctant to give up part of a loved one's eyes, and need some incentive."

Nadia thought, *The dead don't need their eyes anymore. I desperately need them, and I've tried and tried everything else!*

Nadia stared at Dr. Bella, and said, "I will be happy to put up some money for an incentive right now. How much do you think it will take?"

"$20,000 American dollars. It needs to be cash. It will be worth it; you are getting the best possible care from now on," Dr. Bella assured her. "Replacing an opaque cornea is the *only* way to restore clear vision after it becomes so damaged."

"Then what?" Nadia asked.

"When a donor becomes available, you will come here and we will give you medication to relax you and keep you from feeling any pain. Then I will cut small circles from the clear parts of your eyes, your corneas. I will transplant small circles of the donated corneas, called buttons, using fine suture material, one-fourth the thickness of a human hair. Using an operating microscope, I will sew the new corneas into place!"

"That sounds fine. Can I go back to the States right afterwards?"

"No. You will have to stay here for six weeks for suture removal, and steroid eye drops. I must keep tabs on your progress. We have to be ready to prevent the rejection by the body of the donated material."

Nadia shrugged, "Okay, I guess. How long do you think it will be before a donor is available?"

"If you have cash, it won't take long."

CHAPTER 16
THE INFORMAL INVESTIGATION

Manuel was in his kitchen, perched on a stool, talking on the phone with the Ministry of Health in Guadalajara.

He spoke into the receiver angrily, "You can't keep putting this off! The American Embassy informed your office that Dr. Bella has committed serious malpractice against children about a month ago. Surely *some* evidence has turned up – unless there has been no investigation."

The ministry of Health department clerk finally sighed and said, "*Uno momento.*"

Manuel waited, pushing his thick black hair back, expecting to be disconnected again. At last, another male voice answered the phone. He introduced himself as the supervisor, and said, "If such allegations had any possible basis in fact, we would have informed the hospital and the Guadalajara police. We keep records of all complaints and we conduct our own investigations as well. If you have a legitimate need to know and any right to further information, you will need to speak to the police, and the hospital administrators in person."

Manuel slammed the phone down, growling, "That's just perfect!"

He began to pace the floor. He had a family and two businesses to run. His wife had two businesses to run as well: the clothing shop, and the resort. Manuel again sat and picked up the phone to enlist police chief García's help, as Victor had once suggested.

When the Chief García heard Manuel's request to go with him to Guadalajara, he said, "You know, I've been hoping one of you would ask me for help."

Chief García felt guilty about the leak to the media concerning Javier's kidnapping because he had told a few policemen buddies about it, after his fourth Tecate with lime and tequila chaser. They had laughed and howled like hyenas about Javier being dropped off in his underwear after the kidnapping. Perhaps one of the policemen, hungry for a little spending money, offered the news to competing news reporters.

García continued, "If you speak with my police officers in Guadalajara, Manuel, be careful not to offend them. My superintendant is there. We must be sociable and patient."

"Okay. I will follow your lead. You're the bullfighter, and I am the clown. If the bull chases us and strikes, the horns will stick in my rear end, not yours."

"Ha! I wish!"

The next day, Chief García rode with Manuel over to Guadalajara, to visit the police officers and the superintendant. The Guadalajara police headquarters' main office was furnished with antique phones, dented file cabinets, and graying linoleum floors. Windows were open to the pleasantly cool, January air that was

141

beginning to warm with the afternoon. A black, overhead fan swirled slowly. Several police officers had gathered, eager to see Chief García. Some were sitting on the edges of cluttered desks, and others were in the oversized, black, artificial leather chairs. A couple were drinking Cokes and smoking cigarettes. Only one was busily filling in some forms at his desk.

The chief of Guadalajara had a heavy, low forehead, and thoughtful eyes, which fixated on Manuel, as if taking his measure. He offered Manuel and Chief García each a cold Coke.

After getting comfortably seated, and exchanging pleasantries, general news, and conversations about health, at last the conversation turned to business.

García said, "Any progress has been made on the investigation of Dr. Bella?"

The chief of Guadalajara folded his hands on the desk in front of him, and said, "Yeah. The American Embassy was whining about Dr. Bella taking some kid's eyes out, so we had some officers follow her and her money around a bit. Her salary from the hospital and the clinics wouldn't cover the two mansions that we've seen so far. Plus, she just bought her mother a house!"

Manuel asked, "Have you and your men investigated where the money *came* from yet?"

The Guadalajara chief's lips grew tight, "No."

García smiled his smooth drinking-buddy smile and said, "Well, at least you found excess money – that's evidence. I am damn upset about the damage she is doing to our children around Puerto Vallarta and in the mountain villages around here. I am sure you are, too. So, can we help? Manuel here knows the boy who got the correct diagnosis in America and who kept the eye she wanted to remove."

"We haven't had any other complaints."

"You're telling me that you have heard *no* other complaints about her?"

"None."

García pulled on his thick, black mustache nervously, glancing at Manuel.

The Guadalajara police officers looked at each other blankly and shook their heads. A few began to drift off.

The chief of Guadalajara stood up. "We'll look for more evidence. We will make a point of asking questions of the villagers with children. Thank you for coming in."

Chief García glanced at Manuel, who nodded and they both stood up.

García said to the chief of the Guadalajara police, "La doctora has grateful, rich, and powerful patients. You might check if any tourists have been seen by Dr. Bella."

The chief of Guadalajara said, "Certainly." He put his mirrored sunglasses on, and then crossed his arms, ending the conversation.

Manuel visited Victor later that day at his noisy newspaper office in Puerto Vallarta to ask him for help. Victor took a lunch break and they walked together to Victor's favorite tamale stand. It was fragrant, with steam from the tamales billowing into the air of the building's blue shadows.

Victor smiled and said, "I got one of my reporters to ask around at the pharmacies about Dr. Bella." Then he bit into a juicy tamale with eyes half-closed with pleasure.

Manuel smiled. "And they found out something, didn't they?" He peeled the paper and corn leaves back slowly.

"Dr. Bella ordered an eye bank set, including corneal section scissors. There are rumors that she did cataract surgeries and corneal implants on rich foreigners. Hard to confirm those statements though. No one wants to point the finger publicly. Also, a couple of the pharmacies sell Dr. Bella's eye drops. Nothing in them but salt water and some preservatives. Harmless, unless someone's been led to expect more."

Manuel nodded. He thought, *could this be what was prescribed for infections when Dr. Bella didn't want the infection to clear*? He didn't need to say it; he could see that Victor already knew by the grim look that passed over his face.

Victor said, "I'm going to Telmex later tonight. A smart guy, U.S. educated, connected to Salinas de Gotari; the whole bit, owes me a favor. He's got our lovely doctor's office and home call records."

"Nice!" Manuel said. Then while wiping his mouth, he eyed the young girl selling the tamales. She reminded him of Audrey, back when she sold tamales after they were first married. He sighed.

Victor mistook the sigh for restlessness to be back at work. He stood up. "Well, good buddy, I'll call you later, direct from the phone company."

He laughed and Manuel joined in.

The Federal District was almost empty by 9pm. The burly night watchmen and several young secretaries, carrying their pastel handbags, greeted Victor, who was wearing his usual captivating grin and a high-quality, gray suit.

The impressive office, with its Aztec-inspired urns and statues and a blend of modern and antique furnishings was certainly nice. Too nice.

Two secretaries smiled at him flirtatiously as they went out the door. He, in turn, watched their behinds appreciatively as they twitched out the building in their heels. He called one back, a secretary with streaked or frosted hair; Victor wasn't sure what they called it these days, to call for his friend who was in the building. She tapped her long, red nails on the counter, unhappy that her duties for the night weren't quite over.

When she hung up, she said, "It's a little late to be visiting."

"Hector just wants to show me the pool table before we go for a beer."

Hector appeared, looking like the clean-shaven, young college graduate that he was. The influence that his years in an American college had was evident. He wore tennis shoes, slacks, and a yellow Hawaiian shirt.

"Hi," he said to Victor. To the secretary, he said, "Don't worry, I'll make sure it stays locked. It's okay. You can go."

The secretary stood up, uncertainly.

Victor intervened. "It's a beautiful night, and a beautiful girl like yourself should be out in it."

She laughed, and soon she was gone.

Victor and Hector went up the elevator and through the carpeted corridors to his friend's office in Telmex. Hector remarked, "It's not like I'm giving away state secrets or anything." For a while, the only sound was the shuffle of their shoes were on the soft carpet. Then he said, "Here it is." He pointed to a computer monitor, and the copies of monthly call records Hector had copied from the microfilms. "Whatever's not in the microfilm, we can bring up on computer. We're sort of between systems right now,

146

trying to store more on the computer and in discs but we still have the old ways."

Victor agreed, "The newspaper also needs a new system to keep track of what we print. Gotta keep track of the lies somehow." He sat down and began to study the lists of what Hector said were Dr. Bella's incoming calls.

Hector pulled up a chair. He said, "The doctor gets calls from the Vallarta clinic, and from clinics in outlying villages, both near the sea and up in the mountains. This is the code for the villages," he pointed. Turning a page, he pointed again, explaining, "She also gets calls from expensive hotels and neighborhoods in Puerto Vallarta and Guadalajara. These digits tell you it's a hotel. That code is the rich district by the beach. See that? Those numbers means she gets many calls from public telephones."

Victor said, "That means that a large number of poor people are calling her."

Hector agreed. He added, "The calls from the Vallarta clinic are easier to analyze than the calls from the hospital in Guadalajara. People would be sharing the phones in the hospital."

While underlining suspicious looking numbers, especially the frequent calls to the United States, Victor said, "Doctor Bella's like our president, Salinas de Gotari. She strongly believes in trading with the United States!"

Hector laughed. "Keep working. I gotta clear out of here. If you need anything from the computer, get it now. The rest you can take."

Victor nodded. He was reminded of the times he had illegally traded with the *Estados Unidos* transporting goods back to Mexico in the back of a truck when he was in his early twenties. He had often said, "Hell, I do better business out of the back of my car than most stores on the street fronts. You don't hear me say, There isn't any." Now Victor saw that Dr. Bella was doing the same thing, in her own, horrible way.

"May I call someone before I go?" He asked.

"Yeah. Keep it short."

He said to the maid who answered, "Please let me speak to Javier? Yes, I'll wait." It's easy to get in touch with a man who no longer has to work, he thought. You just have to wait for him to return from his bath, or swim, or his boat – he's always in the water somewhere. He examined his shiny, buffed fingernails.

"Victor! How's things? What can I do for you?" Javier said.

"Pretty good. I'm looking at the phone records of doctor Dr. Bella. I was wondering if you could hire some men to follow her."

"No problem. Whatever you say. I had a lot of time to think while those bodyguards kept me prisoner. I owe both you and my brother this favor. Besides, my brother is fond of Julian. I hired that kid over the summer you know, a good worker."

Victor smiled. "Thank you. How soon do you think you can get on this?"

"Right away."

He hung up and held up a hand to ward off Hector. Then he called Manuel. "Direct hit. Lots of calls that can't be anything other than extra-curricular business. Javier says he'll hire some men to follow her if we want."

Manuel said, "Good job on the phone numbers. I have to get back to the wife, okay? She's feeling neglected."

Victor and Hector left through the front door of the company. Hector carefully locked the door and set the alarm. Next, they crossed the busy street as buses and cars came careening dangerously near them. Crowds of people also risked crossing between speeding cars as they headed to the town for a bit of fun and some drinks.

Once safely on the sidewalk again, Hector asked Victor. "Something wrong?"

"Now that I see how much business she's doing, I gotta do something, real soon."

Hector frowned. "Don't do anything dangerous, Victor."

"I can't promise you that, but if we stop her, it will be partly thanks to you."

"Sure. See you round okay?"

Victor went home for a bit of sleep at last. This investigation was going to cost him some time, there was no doubt about it.

After a good night's sleep, Victor put on a fresh-smelling, pressed shirt and arrived early at the newspaper's office, just as his chief editor was exclaiming, "The drug cartel leader, Amando Carrillo Fuentes, just died!"

Victor called out, "Drug overdose, or did someone do us all a favor and shoot him?"

The editor hurried over, sweating profusely, "He was having extensive plastic surgery to disguise himself, and he died during the process!"

Victor hung his coat on the back of his chair. "So, there is some justice after all. Print it, but don't offend anyone by revealing what he really was, or why he was having plastic surgery. Most people know what he is and will figure out why he was getting the surgery anyway. It doesn't pay to say everything about drug cartel leaders." he said.

His editor drooped visibly, but nodded in agreement.

That day in February 1997, an article revealing nothing except the death of a well-known, wealthy man who was having plastic surgery was published in *La Journada Mexico.*

After 3pm, Victor drove himself, using the company van, to a barrio on the outskirts of Puerto Vallarta. A small dog barked at him from the dirt road. Victor approached an open door near a clay, outdoor, cook stove. He knocked on the doorframe.

A barefooted boy of about three years of age appeared at the door. His too-short, striped shirt revealed his belly button, and his wide, brown eyes looked Victor over.

"¡*Mamá!* Someone rich is here!"

Julian's mother, Marisol, came to the door, her hand brushing her hair back. "¿*Sí?*"

"Don't worry, Señora," Victor said, smiling gently. "I am friends with Manuel, and I met your son, Julian, when he was working for Javier. He says Julian is a good worker and a good kid."

Marisol blushed. "Please come in, Señor."

She showed him to a well-worn wooden table. A refreshing, tropical air blew through the house. A small dish of Nasturtiums graced the table, alongside a bowl of avocados and tomatoes.

"Please forgive my plain house. Can I get you some horchata?"

Victor accepted the drink, saying, "To your health!" and he raised it toward her a bit in a toast. "Your home is clean and pretty!" *And so are you!*, he thought.

She sat down on the edge of a hard chair. She was about thirty years old. Her thick, black hair was coiled up and loose strands fell about her long neck. Victor admired her muscular arms and full bosom, framed by a colorful, embroidered blouse.

"How is Javier's health?" Marisol asked.

Victor thought, *He's been a nervous wreck and grouchier than usual, but he seems to appreciate everyone more – except his wife.* Victor answered, "Javier will be fine. His wife is taking good care of him. Manuel and I are concerned that Dr. Bella is still practicing medicine on young people such as your son and his girlfriend. What was her name?"

"María."

"How is Julian now?" Victor asked.

Marisol answered. "He's back in school. His left eye, the hurt one, looks the wrong way, but he says it doesn't bother him." She shook her head and smiled.

"Is he doing well in school?"

She sighed and remained silent, studying his face.

"What's wrong?"

"Well, I can't get him to do his homework, or eat, or go out with his friends."

"Sounds like he's upset. Any idea why?"

"He hates Dr. Bella, hates his life, says he's ugly. He hates the police, says they never do anything but harass the poor and serve the rich."

Victor nodded. "I know just how he feels. He's mad as hell and won't feel better until he can do something about her. I can tell you are a good mother."

Marisol waited.

He continued, "I know this will scare you, but I must ask you to let Julian help us catch her. She doesn't know that he has been treated in the United States. I'm sure she would still recommend that he have his eye removed if she thinks you don't know any better."

Marisol stood up, backed toward her sink and crossed her arms. "No! You can't use my son to turn in this doctor."

Victor forced himself to stay seated. He could keep himself sounding calmer if he did, and it would be harder for Marisol to push him out of the house if he was sitting in the chair she had offered him, drinking the drink she gave him. The glass was empty now, though.

He said, "It would help Julian to feel alive again. He wouldn't feel helpless anymore. Boys are like this. His father would have understood. Manuel and I wouldn't let her do anything to him."

He wondered however, *Can I truly assure his safety? Would the police really do anything if she were caught red-handed?*

Marisol pressed her hands to her temples. "You didn't know Julian's father! I need Julian here! No one takes my son away for anything that might be dangerous. Catch her some other way."

"I could run articles about her, but I could lose my business that way. That would be better than causing any harm to your son, though."

Marisol softened.

He tried again. "If she says that Julian still needs his eye removed, the police will have to put her in jail. They would be embarrassed *not* to put her in jail."

Victor stood, relieved to get his large frame off the small, hard wooden chair. He went to Marisol, took her delicate hand in his, raised it to his lips, and kissed it.

He said, "Señora, I am not truly a good man. I never had a wife or raised fine sons such as you have, so I am sure I have no right to ask you to consider this. I can't truly understand how you must feel. I do love children, though. And I hate to know that they are being hurt like this in my own beloved country. I've never done anything worthy at all, except when I helped a little bit to bring Javier back to his family. It felt good to be some help.

"Now I want to stop *la doctora* from hurting any more children. I feel strongly about this. Ask Julian how he feels about helping to put her in jail. You know that he is becoming a man. Will you think about it, *Mamacita*?"

His eyes sparkled like the jewelry the vendors set out on black velvet in the marketplace. Marisol felt a feeling she hadn't felt since before her husband lost his will to live and died. His self-deprecating smile tickled her heart.

She said, "All right, I'll talk to him. I agree that we need more justice around here, especially for the ones like María, who have lost so much and have no one to help them."

Marisol watched the Victor drive away until it turned the corner. When she entered her house again, she looked in the small mirror, and was surprised to see herself looking attractive and smiling.

Julian came home from school, late as usual. His little brother was already seated at the wooden table, eating tortillas with beans and drinking water with lime and a little sugar in it. Enrique's elbows, which were on the table again, were covered with scratches from crawling under porches with the neighbor's dogs and his friends. Marisol stood at the table over him, her hands in a bowl of squishy corn masa.

"*¡Hola, Mamá!*" Julian called and came to give her a kiss on the cheek.

She said, "Why are you late?" Then she began smearing the dough onto cornhusk leaves.

"*Mamá,* if I come right home, I never have any fun. What is the point of living if we just work all of the time?"

"If you do well in school, you won't have to work all of the time, *hijo.* Get some beans from the pot. Tortillas and avocados are on the table." She put a few spoonfuls of cooked chicken in the center of each coated leaf.

"What were you doing that was so fun?" she asked.

"Playing video games with Ricky."

Marisol thought, *I wonder why he doesn't seem to be interested in much of anything lately, besides electronic games? That man, what was his name? He had said something about Julian needing to help stop Dr. Bella in order to stop feeling powerless.*

Her son was becoming as handsome as his father was, although his blind eye didn't look directly at her. It changed his appearance a little. He looked tough now, as if he had been in a fight. She recalled Manuel and Audrey assuring her that the American doctors would make his eye see again in a few years. She hoped that was true.

"Do you have any homework today?" she asked.

"No," he answered absently while he helped himself in to a fourth tortilla. After he finished eating and drinking, he put his glass in the tub of soapy water she had left in the sink. He went to the bedroom, which was also their living room, turned on the new television in the main room and began pressing little buttons to shoot at cartoon creatures.

Marisol placed the tamales into a pot to steam. She remembered, *He used to have homework last year.* She sighed, thinking, *Report cards in a couple days, then I'll see if he is doing his homework. I hope so, or the Todds will be angry.*

Later, she had to leave the house and bring most of the tamales to the tourists who stayed in the big houses in Conchas Chinas. She called to Julian, "Take care of your brother. Let him play some games, too."

"Oh, okay Mama," he said.

Enrique came running up to Marisol and hugged her around her thighs. "Don't go, Mama!" he cried.

Marisol kissed him on the forehead and left.

Two days later, Manuel visited Marisol's house. Manuel, Marisol, and Julian were all crowded into the small kitchen, which seemed smaller than ever to Julian at the moment. Electric light shone from a single bulb, which hung from the center of the ceiling, making Julian feel overheated and on display. Marisol stood by, nervously pinching her apron into creases, watching as Manuel questioned her son, as she had done earlier - to no effect.

Manuel demanded of Julian "How do you explain these grades?"

Julian hung his head and didn't answer.

Manuel waved the report card emphatically, "Your mother works hard to support you, and the Todds send money so that you can go to school... This is how you repay everyone? We are all very upset. Mr. Todd wants me to take all the games away from you, which is what I am going to do."

The two adults stared at Julian, waiting for any response. Julian listened to the game noises that Enrique was making. He wondered what pitiful score his little brother had gotten.

Manuel said, "He's not even listening. Those games need to go! Marisol, look, Julian needs something to do that reflects that he is becoming a man. Of course, you are afraid to let Julian help with convicting Dr. Bella, but do you want Julian to get his sense of purpose back? Do you want justice? We have a better chance of making a case against Dr. Bella if we catch her in a purposeful misdiagnosis. For that, we need Julian."

Overhearing this, Julian felt as if the Blessed Mary had walked into the room at that very moment just to save him! Anything that would get the focus off of his grades was welcome.

He said, "Mama, I want to help catch her, more than anything!"

Marisol was upset that Manuel brought this up in front of Julian, knowing that now Julian would be pleading with her relentlessly. She said, "His father wanted him to do well in school, not to chase criminals." she countered.

"He could do both," Manuel asserted as he began unplugging and carrying out the TV, VCR, and the Nintendo 64 equipment. "He could start preparing to be a man, like his father would have wanted him to."

It bothered Manuel that his own boy also played with these games so much at home, but he allowed it as long as Ricky kept his grades up. His shoulder blades jerked visibly under his shirt as he irritably pulled cords out of consoles. He was frustrated with teenagers in general tonight, and upset about Dr. Bella. His leather shoes grated harshly on the gritty floor as he carried most of the entertainment in Julian's home out the door.

Julian watched, feeling misunderstood, but he didn't dare open his mouth or even rise from his chair lest the grown-ups start in on him again about not doing his schoolwork. He did feel bad about being so lazy, but school was so boring and pointless.

Enrique had a crying fit about the games going away, which didn't help anyone's mood.

Marisol remembered that Julian had been babysitting Enrique during most of his free time, like a grandmother, and playing with these American toys. She felt remorseful suddenly, for neglecting Julian in a way she couldn't help. When her husband was healthy and strong, he had always steered the family with a warm touch. She imagined that she felt his reassuring hand on her now, and so she put her hand on Julian's shoulder. She spoke what she believed her husband would have said, "Son, I know you didn't mean to let things go so badly."

Julian raised his eyes and looked at her. Finally, he looked sorry for hurting her.

An extended family of some kind was needed to do a proper job with children, Marisol felt. Perhaps Manuel was right; she was keeping Julian from becoming the man he could be if she did not let him help. He needed male role models, so if Manuel insisted he do his homework, and assured her that Julian would be safe, perhaps Julian could help them.

After slamming the back of his van shut, Manuel returned to the rough stucco doorway. Enrique was hanging on to his mother's skirt, and Marisol had a hand on each of her boys. Manuel empathized with her huge task.

"Let me work with the boy for awhile," he pleaded one last time. "I will ensure that he gets his school work done and that he is safe."

"*Sí*, perhaps it is best," she agreed.

Julian's form took on life, unfurling from the hunched, slumped position to cheerful attention.

"Really Mama?" he looked up at her.

She nodded, eyes wet with tears.

Manuel was euphoric as he rattled up the cobblestone street in his rapidly decaying van toward his home. A piece of the puzzle of the meaning of his life was falling into place.

CHAPTER 17 A STRANGE DATE

Julian wondered if a miracle had occurred and María's brown eyes could see him. She moved easily as she sewed the garments, with the sun from a nearby window warming her back. She had opened the door herself, and had led him back to where she was sitting and had easily picked up and continued her work. She was crocheting something white. Her smile was warm and she teased him gently, but Julian was answering automatically. He only saw her backlit hair glowing like the Virgin of Guadalupe, or at least an angel.

She said, "Thank you for all that money you gave us. I got a tutor, and a lady who taught me how to get around."

"There was extra money you mean, after your mom paid for the new eyes?"

"No. The hospital didn't charge anything for the eyes. That lady doctor was lying about them costing $300."

"Oh." He had worked so hard to give her eyes that she could have gotten for free!

A little grouchily, Julian asked her what the tutor did.

"You know Julian, after I got these "eyes", I still couldn't see. I had to relearn how to do everything. I even learned how to read with my hands! That was because of you. Mama wouldn't have even taken me in the first place to get the eyes, if it weren't for you, because she thought it cost too much."

161

Julian had achieved more than he had ever dreamed.

Softly, María asked, "Why did you give me so much money, Julian?"

Julian hadn't really thought about it. He had just wanted to do something to make himself feel better. Perhaps by helping María, he was fighting the darkness that was stealing their sight, their lives, their peace.

"I just wanted you to be happy again," he said at last.

She smiled in his direction and then nodded at the fluffy pile on her lap, "I am making this for my quinceañera. She draped one side of the lace over her hair and face, "Do you think it will look all right on me?"

He smiled. "Yeah, you will look good all right. When is your *quinceañera*?"

"In a month."

"Well, can you come out before then? Would you like to walk by the beach? I could buy you a Popsicle, and we could look around the plaza...." He suddenly felt very uncomfortable. He felt sweat form in his newly forming, fuzzy mustache. He wiped the sweat with his finger and thumb, copying the spreading motion that men with full mustaches used.

María wrapped the delicate white yarn around the crochet needle, and pulled it through. She stopped, and looked his way, "I wish I could, Julian. You would have to hold my hand, though. It wouldn't look right. You know that, don't you?"

Julian realized that she was correct. He said, "I guess I better ask your mother. Maybe Esther could come with us."

María giggled with delight at the idea. She called out, "Mamá, Julian has something he wants to ask you."

Julian wanted to kick her gently and shush her, but it didn't seem right to kick a blind person – even if you are half-blind yourself. When Rosa appeared, Julian shyly raised his eyes, "*Señora, por favor*, would you let me take María out to the beach and the plaza? We could ask Esther to come along."

Rosa beamed with pleasure at Julian's invitation, "*Claro*. Of course."

Rosa insisted upon walking with them immediately to Esther's house. She spoke to Esther's oldest brother, because her father was out with the sheep. The oldest brother assured them that Esther would meet them tomorrow after school, as soon as her homework was done. Julian remembered then that he too, needed to start being conscientious about his homework.

The next day, the three friends went to a movie, *The Rock*, with Spanish subtitles. They splurged on lemonade and popcorn with hot sauce. Esther was helpful with María, leading her to the women's room and taking turns reading the subtitles to María.

Esther and María kept their arms linked even during the movie. Julian longed for some of that contact. Esther was beautiful, and it was natural that they exchanged glances around María. He was also proud of the brave, graceful way María went along with this idea. He briefly touched María's hand as it rested on the armrest between them in the semi-darkness of the theater. He felt a current of life, or love, coming from her skin.

Then he worried for a moment that Ricky would be upset that he hadn't been invited. *"Why didn't I invite him?"* Julian wondered. Julian used to think that he would be with Esther someday because she was tall, shapely, and calm. Ricky had liked spunky, playful María. In the boy's minds, Julian had been informally "with" Esther since he was tall and Esther was physically mature. Ricky was maturing slowly and María was younger, so they had been considered "together", even though none of the children had spoken of it, kissed, or even held hands. Now, Esther was planning to get married, which changed everything.

When he dropped the two girls off at Esther's house, María smiled radiantly. She said, "That was the most fun I've had in a long time. Thank you."

"Yeah. That was a fun movie."

"I like the way you read, Julian – with feeling!" She giggled.

Julian blushed. He had read with feeling in order to make it interesting for her. He had even tried to sound like the different characters. Esther had given a straight reading. She was a good student, but she never cared much for reading, and was too reserved to read with feeling.

Esther reopened the door, and pulled María into her house, "Good-bye Julian. Thank you," she called.

As soon as Esther shut the door, she began to whisper, "He kept looking at your face and your hand during the movie."

María's fingers went instinctively up to her eyebrow and lightly touched the white scar there that divided her eyebrow slightly.

Esther saw that María was taking this wrong, so she said more plainly, "He likes you!"

"Really?"

Esther practically jumped up and down. "I *know* about these things! Do you know how lucky you are?"

María brought the crucifix around her neck up to her lips and kissed it.

CHAPTER 18 AUDREY

Audrey wanted to take care of her own life and forget Dr. Bella. After all, Julian was fine wasn't he? In her own tastefully decorated bedroom, life was so orderly. She put her hairbrush down on the carved vanity table, "You're not still going to go after Dr. Bella, are you?"

"Well, I still want to do it," Manuel said, buttoning his dark blue shirt.

"But, are you still going to take Julian and Victor to Guadalajara?"

"There is only one way I can. And it depends entirely on you. Can you handle the resort, and answer questions at the lumber yard while I'm gone?"

"I can, but I want to forget about it and just get on with our lives. Don't we have plenty of problems of our own, just trying to hold on to what we have?" She hugged him and he held her. Over his shoulder, she stared at her diamond wedding ring. She wanted her husband safe. She released him, and he went to the bathroom.

Someone should stop Dr. Bella, but did it have to involve her husband? The children in the impoverished hills around Guadalajara and Puerto Vallarta whom Dr. Bella had blinded, especially María, deserved it. That girl used to have such expressive, pretty, and observant, eyes. Julian's mother's description of the waiting room full of blind and half-blind children in the mountains of Guadalajara came up before her like a ghost.

Audrey looked at her husband, who had started shaving in the bathroom with the door open, and called out resignedly, "I can do it, but ask Javier to help out with managing the lumberyard, okay?"

He stopped shaving in mid-stroke and smiled at her. "Good idea. My brother will help, I'm sure. That's why I married a smart woman." He undressed again as he approached his wife.

She smiled, holding out her arms with passion.

CHAPTER 19 RUSES

Victor sprawled comfortably on a hotel bed. Manuel said to him, "When you take Julian to the hospital, The doctor will believe you are his uncle only if you act worried and treat Julian with familiarity."

Victor had laughed when he tried to call Julian "nephew."

Julian sat at a table, playing solitaire. Manuel turned to Julian and asked, "What do you want your new *tio's* name to be?"

Julian scratched his head and frowned. He said, "Diego Martinez would be fine. I had a classmate with that name."

Victor got up and strode across the small hotel room like a bullfighter and made a grand bow. "Señor Diego Martinez at your service."

Julian giggled and said, "Say, *Tio*, could you bring me a Coke?"

Manuel laughed, "Guys, get serious." But he smiled and took a slug of coffee.

Julian nodded and then pleaded, "*Grande* uncle Martinez, would you kindly buy me a big gringo car from Tijuana?"

Victor puffed out his chest and said, "I have connections with all the best underground Mafia along the border. What color would you like your Mercedes Benz, my precious nephew?"

Julian got up and took Victor's hand. "Cherry red would be just fine, *Tio*."

Victor said, "You got it." Then Victor dropped Julian's hand and straightened Julian's collar. Next, he wet his thumb with his tongue and wiped some imaginary dirt off of Julian's face.

Manuel laughed and then said, "Victor, you don't have to act like his mother. Okay. Now, before Dr. Bella can get suspicious, get the diagnosis and the medicine and leave as soon as possible. I don't want her to start covering her tracks. Do you remember the symptoms we discussed?"

Julian said, "Itching, painful, red eyes."

Victor tried to force his giant hands into the front pocket of a too-small pair of jeans they had bought off of a farmer. He did a slippery dance in pointy cowboy boots as he tried to pull the small bottle out of the tight pocket. Manuel stifled a laugh. Julian cracked a smile, but turned to cough when Victor glanced at him.

Victor said, "These drops are going to feel a little uncomfortable. They will make your eye red. It's time to put them in your eye now." Then he put drops in Julian's blind eye.

Dr. Bella entered the examination room. Her eyes opened wider when she saw Julian. She said, "I remember you."

Julian was seated in a black chair, which had huge arm-like extensions with lenses on them for measuring eyesight deficiencies. "Hello, Doctor," Julian said.

169

"Buenos tardes Señora Doctora," Victor said, affecting the speech of a rancher. He tipped his white hat. "I am Julian's uncle. I'm afraid Julian needs your help once again."

"What's the matter?" She said, and she looked at Julian's eye.

"My eye has been itching, and it kind of hurts, too."

To Victor, she said, "It looks like a bad case of conjuntivitis. Why didn't his mother bring him?"

"At the clinic in Puerto Vallarta, they said you would be here for a long time, so she asked me to bring him to you. She is afraid to travel so far, and there is the little brother who needs looking after."

Julian watched this scene in its humming florescent light through his one good eye. Victor's colorful plaid shirt stood out compared to against Dr. Bella's white coat.

Victor continued. "His mother took him to the herbalist, but her drops didn't help. His eye still bothers him all of the time lately. His mother needs you to take care of him."

Dr. Bella's sharp eyes focused on his Victor's hands, with their perfect nails, and untanned skin.

Victor continued, "His mother has no…husband." He glanced at Julian. "The father passed on a couple years ago, so she works."

Then Dr. Bella faced Julian, who sat on the table. She said, "Look up," She flashed a small, but bright light into his eye. "Now look down, left…..right." She turned to Victor and said, "His mother should have let me take care of this earlier, but I can still ease the boy's needless discomfort."

She wrote quickly in black ink, then ripped a white sheet of paper off of a pad and handed it to Victor.

"Take this prescription to the pharmacy."

Damn it! That's not much of a false diagnosis. And it's not going to get her in trouble! thought Victor.

CHAPTER 20 THE STAIRS

Carmen Bella swooped into the nurse's station, almost knocking over Emilio, a nurse who stood filling in details of his shift. She grabbed him by the arm and pulled him closer. "I know that boy! His family reported me to the Ministry of Health!"

"So?" He shrugged. "You're not in trouble anyway."

"Yes, but they need to learn to leave me alone."

"What are they up to?"

"Some "uncle" of his brought him in instead of his mother. They need to forget, or wish they had!"

"That's easy enough. Delay them. Don't let them in the elevator."

A nurse put a yellow, plastic cleaning cone in front of the elevator.

"Why can't we go down the elevator the way we came up?" Victor asked her.

"Oh, I'm sorry. Someone just threw up in the elevator and they are cleaning it now. If you wait just a few minutes, it will be ready again. Would you like some coffee?"

"Yes, that would be nice," Victor said. Julian looked at the closed elevator doors and pushed the button anyway. Nothing happened.

After the nurse left, Julian said, "Let's take the stairs."

"You sure you wouldn't rather just wait?"

"Manual said to get out quickly," Julian reminded him. After finding the narrow, winding stairs, Julian took each step slowly with one hand on each wall, while Victor followed him.

It was stuffy, at first, but as they descended a few more floors they could smell fresh air. They could see sunshine and fresh air coming in from an open door below them. When they neared it, two men lunged toward them. One man began strangling Julian. Julian's face turned purple. Victor grabbed the man, and attempted to push him back outside with the parked ambulances. As Julian gasped for air, a man pulled his head down, and dealt him a knee to the head. Julian went unconscious.

The second man crashed a .45 down on Victor's head. Victor crumpled to his knees and put his hands out to break his fall. When he struggled to get up, the huge attacker yelled, "No! Down you go, *cabrón!*" and kicked Victor's ribs. Julian's attacker, a wiry man with a round glasses, pulled Julian out of the emergency exit door, and said to the other, "Quick, get him out here!"

The big man dragged Victor out.

They ordered Victor, at gunpoint, into the back of an ambulance. Then the one with the glasses threw Julian inside. The big man with a hooked nose got in the back with them. Afterwards, another young man appeared and shut the doors. He jumped into the passenger seat. Emilio, the man with the glasses, got in the driver's seat and drove them away from the hospital.

173

CHAPTER 21
MANUEL SEARCHES

"The boy and his uncle left over half an hour ago."

Manuel asked the nurse, "*Por favor*, would you check again?"

He looked out the window and saw that the sun was setting. A white, dark-haired woman with a stunning youthful figure, wearing a leopard print dress and dark sunglasses, entered and received an enthusiastic greeting from the nurse, who immediately escorted her to the examination rooms within. Manuel knew that American women were fond of their sunglasses, none more than his blond wife, but this woman wore hers indoors. He wondered why.

The nurse at the desk declared, "I'm sorry, visiting hours are over."

In the waiting room, a few people waited, eating, sleeping, or bouncing children on their knees. Through the door, he saw a small cafeteria from which several flies darted out.

"But what about these people?" He asked.

"They are waiting to be seen by a doctor," she said, and pointed at a closed door.

Manuel shuffled out of the hospital into the rose-colored sunset, enhanced by smog and haze.

Across the street, were several stores displaying coffins in the windows. Silver and polished wood coffins on shelves were stacked up to the ceilings.

On the hospital's side of the street, was a walled-in alley and a small parking lot. There were numerous dumpsters, parked ambulances, and large, roll-up loading doors.

Manuel saw an arm moving behind a dumpster. He approached, and saw that it was a blond man seated in a silver Lexus, smoking a cigarette.

Manuel watched him for a while, then he approached the back steps of a hospital exit. He looked down at the concrete steps of the main exit door. He saw a smudge of what could have been blood, and black shoe marks. Next, he heard the talking of women approaching the door, and he backed away.

Two nurses supporting the sunglass-wearing woman in the leopard print dress, held the doors open, and all three of them walked slowly to the silver Lexus. Manuel, alert, and charging with adrenaline, raced around to the front of the hospital to get into his truck. *"God, don't let them leave before I can get in position to follow them,"* he prayed. He was gasping for air as he turned the key. His truck roared up the driveway and around the hospital, then he slowed up, and crept around the corner.

The silver car was still there, but the woman didn't appear to be in it. Manuel was momentarily confused. He looked up and down the alley in case she had gone somewhere else. It was now difficult to see, for the sun had just gone down. The driver of the Lexus pulled out. Manuel followed the car through town. The

Lexus was going fast. A few people ran across the streets and Manuel had to swerve to avoid them. He saw the man park the car in front of a popular tourist restaurant. He stopped his truck and watched the man help the woman out of the Lexus.

They entered the restaurant beneath a well-lit sign. Shortly after, Manuel entered. He found the couple in the middle of a large open-air patio at the back of the restaurant, seated by a fountain. The patio was lit by torches; small, white sparkling lights, and candles on the table. *Good, it will be easy to fade into the shadows*, he thought. He asked to be seated at the small table on the other side of the fountain. He waited impatiently for an elderly man, who had eaten his meal, to leave. In the meantime, the couple had been served, and the lithe, blond man was assisting the woman with her food. He cut it for her, and occasionally as she ate, he reached across the table with a napkin to wipe her face.

When Manuel sat near the bubbling fountain, behind the overflowing plants growing both in the water and around it, he noticed the bandages on the woman's eyes, behind her sunglasses. He could just barely hear the conversation, when he leaned inward. The woman gestured with both hands as she spoke.

She said, "Of course Doctor Bella said I should stay here in case of rejection, but really, I can find more and better doctors back in San Diego. You know, David, the part of the operation I could only have done here is over. Any doctor in America can administer the anti-rejection drugs. It's not like anyone's going to do anything, even if they do ask questions!"

"Oh yeah? They most certainly would!"

"Well, nothing would come of it. Besides, I will be able to see well enough to help with the driving day after tomorrow, if that's what you're worried about."

Manuel could not hear the low tones of the man's voice. The woman appeared mollified, but Manuel could not find out what the couple's plans were. If this woman had just received surgery that required a cornea donor, she might know where Julian and Victor had gone. Perhaps there was a secret clinic.

Manuel walked over and interrupted them, "Pardon me, but I couldn't help overhearing that you had seen Dr. Bella. I dropped my friend and a boy off at the hospital earlier today, and now they are missing. He was seen by Dr. Bella, too."

David and Nadia shifted in their seats uncomfortably, and Nadia asked, "So? Is there anything we can do for you?"

He said to David, "I need any kind of help you can give me. My friends, a boy and his uncle didn't come back out of the hospital. The boy needed eye surgery. Is there a special after hours clinic that, you know, they don't want to tell everyone about because of the special prices or something? Dr. Bella has done some special work for my nephew and some of our friends before after hours. They couldn't afford the normal prices."

"I'm sure we don't know anything about them," David said, his eyes became piercing, "What do you want to know exactly?"

"Did your wife have a cornea transplant?"

"Yes. So?"

"Dr. Bella wanted to remove the boy's cornea – the boy who is missing – and there was nothing wrong with his eye."

"Nadia wouldn't take any living child's eye. What do you think the doctor did, kidnap your boy and take his eye by force to give it to her?"

"I am only asking what you both know about Dr. Bella."

Nadia, looking a little like Jackie Onassis would if she had been through a terrible accident and had forgotten how to dress, said, "She is the most compassionate doctor we have found. I was going blind waiting for the other doctors."

Manuel asked, "Why did you come in just when the hospital was closing?"

Nadia smiled tightly, "Dr. Bella said that after 5pm would be the most convenient time, since she is so busy. She's not a machine that shuts off at closing time like those other doctors at the eye banks."

"The doctors at the eye banks wouldn't let you have any of the corneas they stored at the bank?"

Nadia fumbled for a cigarette. David got them each one, lit them both in his mouth, and pressed one to her mouth.

Nadia said to him, "Thank you, baby." To Manuel she said, "You got that right. I'm last on everyone's list, thanks to these little coffin nails, and these fine beverages." She lifted her wine glass in a mock toast.

Manuel pressed on, "Do you know where she gets her donors?"

She answered, "Why of course! She pays the families whose children have just died."

"How do you know this?"

David leaned forward and jutted his chin out, "People die all of the time, and people who need money sell their body parts. ......"

Manuel interrupted, "No! This doctor removes the eyes of children who are *alive*. Many blind children live in the mountains surrounding this city and in Puerto Vallarta because of her!"

Nadia stood up abruptly, "*If* that is true, and I don't believe it, you have a big problem. You need to tell the police. There isn't anything we can do for you."

"Wait! Did you see anyone leave at all? You were in the back of the hospital, waiting for her."

David, his arm around Nadia, ready to lead her out, said in an off-hand way, "The only vehicle that left from behind the hospital was an ambulance."

Manuel followed them, "Would you please tell me where you are staying just in case I –"

"What?"

"In case Dr. Bella needs you to collaborate her story. She may need evidence that she was busy during the kidnapping."

The headwaiter was staring at them when David stopped, "We have nothing to hide. If you need us we will be staying at La Tapatía for a while."

"David!" Nadia exclaimed, "I want to leave!"

Manuel heard them quarreling as he dashed past and ran toward his car. He quickly drove to the dimly lit police emergency door. A guard glared at Manuel. At night, the office looked less casual. The lights showed the stark, worn out edges of the furniture and of the men who worked there. In the background, Manuel could hear the two-way radio, with its continuous reports of crimes in progress, fugitives to watch for, and calls to specific officers. After some tense, sarcastic questioning, Manuel reminded the guard of his prior visit with the chief of police when he had brought his friend, Chief Armando García from Puerto Vallarta.

Now Manuel was given coffee and a chair.

The guard excused himself, went into an office, and closed the door.

A little later, Manuel overheard an officer say, "It checks out. We did find unusually high numbers of juvenile eye removals in Dr. Bella's district."

CHAPTER 22 THE CHASE

The ambulance headed north, toward the border, reducing the likelihood of their driver, Emilio, and their ambulance number being recognized.

Julian, meanwhile, became conscious and cried out. The muscular man with a hooked nose smacked him in the face. Julian looked frantically about for help, but saw only Victor, watching helplessly, and Julian slumped back onto the gurney.

They drove to Aguascalientes, and tried to get gas, but all of the gas stations had closed. Emilio took them to a small, brightly lit Mercado with a pig, a sunrise and a Mexican flag painted on its walls. He parked, got out, told the young man, about nineteen years old, to get out and buy some supplies. The young man brought back packaged sandwiches, soda, cigarettes, two bottles of tequila, and a shovel.

Emilio opened the back of the ambulance, and said, "Break time!"

The big hawk-nosed man got out and closed the door on Julian and Victor. The young man passed packages of cigarettes, the sandwiches, and sodas to his pals.

Julian and Victor suffered from thirst and hunger, tied and trapped in the stuffy heat of the closed ambulance. Emilio sneered at Victor and Julian through the window. He was saying something that Julian and Victor couldn't hear.

Julian whispered hoarsely to Victor, "I think I remember the tall, thin man with a shaved head and small glasses from the clinic in Puerto Vallarta."

Victor regretted bringing Julian into this. He sighed. "He probably works for her."

The doors jerked open.

The large, hawk-nosed man and the young man got in the back of the ambulance. The young man demanded of Julian in a high-pitched voice, "What are you staring at?"

Victor said, "Maybe he's thirsty. Why don't you give the kid a drink?"

The young man said, "How precious. So, you think you have huge *cojones*?" He flicked a cigarette butt into Victor's face, "Scum!"

The big, hawk-nosed man asked the young man, "Alfonzo, how about we give him a chance to prove it before we bury them both? Maybe this one's his little boyfriend."

To Julian, he said, "Thirsty?"

He held the soda over Julian's face, as if to pour it in his mouth. Julian opened his mouth to receive it.

"Look at his mouth – the way he holds it!" He laughed. "You little faggot! Drink this!" and he splashed some Pepsi into his face.

"That's enough fooling around," Emilio told them from the driver's seat. "Let's go!"

182

They must have stayed at a motel somewhere, for the van didn't move and the three men took turns guarding them. Emilio watched them first; he seemed to be the least cruel. He let them use a bucket for the toilet, and gave them some water from a bottle he held. Alfonso, the youngest, guarded them in the middle of the night. He didn't give them anything. He mostly stayed outside the ambulance and smoked. When he did come in, he had nothing but cruel things to say, especially to Julian, "I saw you making eyes at Raúl. You think you're going to get out of this by coming on to him, don't you? You think you're so cute." To Victor he said, "Aren't you getting upset that your little lover is flirting? Or do you think he will get you free as well?"

When the big, hawk-nosed man arrived, he and the young one stayed out for a long time. The ambulance shook as if – Victor didn't want to think about what was happening out there. The two captors spoke in low tones for a while; then the young one sounded more high-pitched and upset. The other was growling. *That must be Raúl*, Victor thought.

When Raúl finally came in, he seemed to be in a bad mood. He fumed for a while, and then he said to Julian, "I bet you have a nice ass. You have a nice mouth. Are you hungry? I can give you something to eat. First, let me see that thing you do with your mouth again. Did you hear me?" He slapped Julian. "Do it!" he yelled. He unzipped his pants.

Victor said, "Hey, come on. He's just a kid."

Raúl delivered a kick to Victor's stomach. "Just watch."

Victor lunged at the exposed man. His hands, still tied together at the wrists, he used like a huge claw pulling down its prey. But Raúl was an enormous, strong man, and Victor was tied. Raúl jammed his meaty hands into Victor's neck and choked him. Victor stopped fighting and lay gasping for air.

"Open your mouth," Raúl shouted at Julian, but he shook his head, keeping his mouth closed.

Raúl grabbed Julian's head and crashed it against the side of the ambulance, "You think I can't make you? Fine, I'm going in the back way." He undid Julian's pants despite Julian's struggles. He turned Julian's naked backside to him. Julian bent over, surprisingly – without a fight. Victor saw a slight movement of Julian's hand near his private parts within his pants.

Victor forced his eyes away from Julian. He felt sick suddenly. However, he couldn't stop himself from watching Raúl, who was rubbing his penis, when he heard an explosion. Suddenly the large man was crumpling to the floor of the ambulance, sliding down the inside of the rear door. Then, Victor saw the black gun in Julian's trembling hand. Julian, whose cheek was still bleeding from being smashed into the metal interior, continued to glare crazily at the slumped figure of Raúl, and pointing the gun at him.

In minutes, the other two, having heard the shot in the back of the ambulance, ran to the van and pulled it open.

Alfonzo cried, pointing at Julian, "Emilio, he shot Raúl! Kill him for that!"

Emilio commanded, "Later! Take his gun, and get in! We have to get out of here!"

The ambulance rattled as it careened through early morning traffic, its stinking black smoke, and graffiti-covered colonial buildings on either side. Victor watched the early morning scene of such normality recede from him along with his own former life. Handwritten signs advertised tamales and watermelon juice. He was so thirsty and hungry. A walking policeman in the road tooted his whistle at traffic violations. If only Victor could get his attention. He glanced at Julian to see if he was thinking about this too, but Julian seemed far away.

"Get out of the way!" Emilio yelled at a taxi, which was speeding through a stoplight in front of the ambulance. The brakes screeched, but the ambulance smashed the passenger side of the taxi.

Then Emilio jammed on the accelerator, swerving away from the taxi. "You fat, stupid fool!" He shouted.

The taxi driver followed. Emilio whipped the van to the right, hoping to get out of the congested *el centro*.

A policeman sitting in his marked car stopped eating his tamale, and stared at the taxi, which was chasing the ambulance. The policeman roared after the taxi, lights and sirens coming on, to the gratification of the taxi driver.

The taxi driver shouted, "It's about stinking time you lazy police did something about the *loco* drivers!" Although he had himself run a stop sign moments before the ambulance sideswiped him.

Alfonzo began to whimper through the window that connected the cab to the patient holding area. "Raúl is hurt bad. Let's stop now. It's hopeless. Just tell them that she threatened us. We can't protect her now anyway – they're going to find out everything!"

"Shut up! We can go farther than they can – we have more gas. I'm driving up to the hills. I'll lose them," Emilio shouted back. The three cars ripped out of the narrow city streets and into the outlying farmlands.

It was a straight drive through farmlands for a few miles, before the mountains began. The caravan took on a surreal appearance, with the taxi speeding and swerving between the ambulance and the police. The speeding ambulance was strangely silent.

The houses and farms, surrounded by yellowed, autumn grass, seemed to be a yellow blur to Victor. Broken pottery around the barns sent flashing glints of light through the windows of the ambulance. Bright advertisements such as "¡*Bebe Yahoo!*" flashed by like a kaleidoscope's colored designs.

A barking dog chased the police car for a while. Diego liked dogs and was a little worried that the dog would be hurt, but he sped up and tried to pass the taxi.

The policeman, named Diego, radioed the Aguascalientes department, "*Sí* Señor, I am following a taxi and an ambulance, and both refuse to stop. *Necesito el asistimiento*. Help, *ahora*! We are heading northeast on Valle de las Uvas."

The ambulance drove into the Sierra Madre Occidental, where the jungle grew thick, and villagers were few. The road was becoming as twisted as a grapevine.

Diego's squad car was beginning to overheat. He radioed the police force in León, "If you have a police jeep or off-road vehicle, send a couple of men in it *pronto*! We are headed east."

The taxi, scraping its oil pan, damaging the bumpers and wheel wells, turned back as though it were a beaten fighter. Diego decided to pursue the strange, silent, speeding ambulance.

Meanwhile, Victor gripped the seat legs as the van lurched again over potholes and rocks. Gravel had replaced asphalt miles back, and was now giving way to rutted dirt. Julian hugged the gurney to reduce the pressure from the ropes that bound him.

Victor watched Raúl wince with pain as the ambulance bounced and heaved. Alfonzo stared at the police car through the rear window.

They careened the twisted road through forested mountains. Victor heard more sirens. The León or Aguascalientes policía must be arriving. Moments later, he heard gunshots. Bullets ricochet off the ambulance loudly. The ambulance reeled like a drunken sailor, pounded the ground, lifted up off the road, and overturned.

Victor was tossed about with wild-eyed Julian, the oxygen tanks, the gurney, and the other three screaming men.

The sirens sounded closer.

Everything stopped. Emilio and Alfonzo climbed out of the passenger window. Emilio opened the back door, waved a gun, and screamed, "¡*Vámanos!* Let's go!"

Alfonzo got up, but Raúl just shook his head and waved him away.

"He won't get up!" Alonzo cried.

"Then come on. Leave him!"

"No! I can't leave him," Alfonzo blurted out, and pointed the gun at Julian, "This is your fault!"

Julian's head was bleeding again. He and Victor staggered to their feet.

Emilio shouted, "Don't be stupid! You wouldn't survive prison, little faggot! Let's go!"

CHAPTER 23 THE RÍVER HUNT

"¡*Madre de Dios!* Are you okay?" Diego asked Raúl.

Raúl groaned and swore softly.

Diego held his gun tightly as he went back to the wreck of the ambulance to look for the driver. There was no one in the mangled cab. He called back into the back of the ambulance, "Where is the driver? Who else was here?"

"Figure it out yourself!"

Diego spoke into his radio, "Send an ambulance or two to the Sierra Madre Highway, thirty miles out of Aguascalientes. Internal bleeding, gunshot. One vehicle on its side."

A confirmation came through the radio and Diego could hear more sirens approaching.

Diego cocked his gun and warily looked toward a rocky outcrop in the jungle. He heard movement in the trees.

Just then, the other police cars began arriving like a storm. Officers poured out of their cars. All began asking Diego what happened and were there any dangerous elements loose.

"Take care of this injury here." Diego said and asked, "Did anyone bring a dog?"

"*Sí, aquí está,*" and one of the officers jogged over to him with his dog.

Diego pointed out the places where the others must have been sitting. The dog sniffed the ambulance interior, and the handler led the dog to the driver's seat and the dog sniffed that. Diego saw a cracked, half buried bottle of tequila, leaking its contents into the mud, and a shovel.

The dog began pull at the leash, barking loudly.

The dog's handler said, "The dog knows where they went."

Just then, Manuel arrived with two officers from Guadalajara.

Diego called, "*Vámonos* – come on! Let's get them!"

Manuel jumped out of the black and white police truck. "Wait! Two of the missing men are like my family! They were kidnapped!"

Diego fixed his eyes firmly on Manuel's, "Do you want to come?"

Diego looked at his fellow officers, many of whom were from unfamiliar departments. No one objected.

"All right, let's go!"

Diego and Manuel took off running with four police officers and the dog handler over the rocky outcropping.

The dog led them through a jungle and the brush was thick. They had traveled about a mile, when they came to a small creek in a green, thickly wooded area. Here, the dog lost the scent, and began pacing alongside the creek.

Diego said, "You with the dog, stay around here and see if the dog can pick up the scent again. I'm going to follow down the stream. Who is coming with me?"

"I am," a young officer said.

"Me too," said Manuel.

While walking along the stream, Diego spotted two impressions in the mud. He pointed them out to Manuel and the young officer, "Looks like someone just stopped to take a drink. We're on the right track."

CHAPTER 24 SHOWDOWN

Julian was dehydrated, overheated, and hungry. Keeping up with the other three men was difficult. He looked for ways to steal the gun back and to escape. He fell down into the stream, face first, deliberately, and took a good long drink.

"Get your ass up!" Emilio shouted, delivering a rib cracking kick.

Julian got up, noticing Victor's look of alarm, he forced a smile as if to say, "That was nothing."

They began to run again.

"Look, a house!" Alfonzo shouted.

"*¿Y qué?*" snarled Emilio.

"Steal a truck and escape!"

Emilio and Alfonzo looked at each other.

Julian saw a tidy house, about a mile in from the river, with a wide cement porch, cultivated fields of corn ready for harvesting, but no truck – only a tractor. Perhaps the family had gone to town. That would mean no one to help them, but also that perhaps no one else would get hurt.

Emilio said, "We're going. You," he pointed at Julian, "will knock on the door. Now come on."

Julian hustled to the front porch and waited while the others hid.

"Knock!" Emilio commanded.

There was no answer.

"Knock again! Harder!"

Still no answer.

"Open the door!"

It was not locked.

"Everyone get inside," Emilio ordered, "You first," he pointed at Julian again.

Julian stepped gingerly in, afraid that a sleeping grandmother would wake up and scream.

"Search the house," Emilio told Alfonzo, "Here, take this gun."

Julian watched the gun he had stolen from Javier Neri's home as Alfonzo found his grip on it. Emilio still had his own gun trained on Julian and Victor. Alfonzo went to the back of the house.

Through the window, Julian saw motion near the river. Police!

Emilio turned around to see what Julian was looking at.

Victor grabbed a small television set and crashed it onto Emilio's head. The gun went off, shooting out the window.

Julian heard police shouting. Alfonzo would be back any second with Javier's gun. Julian grabbed Emilio's gun.

From outside, Diego shouted, "Come out now. Give yourselves up."

Alfonzo dashed into the room. He cried, "You again! You're not worth the trouble!"

He pulled the trigger and shot Julian, "That's for Raúl!"

Julian felt hot pain crashing through his arm. He dropped the gun.

"You're next!" Alfonzo shouted at Victor.

Emilio shuttled over and snatched his gun that Julian had dropped from off the floor.

But at that moment, Diego appeared in the window. He shouted at Emilio and Alfonzo, "Halt!"

Emilio shot at Diego and missed.

Diego shot back.

An explosion occurred in the gun; it blew apart. Diego cried out, and dropped the broken gun's parts. Diego's hand was torn open and bleeding.

Julian thought he heard Manuel's voice calling his name. He stepped back, feeling dizzy.

"Come to me!" Manuel whispered from the door.

At that moment, another policeman shouted a warning through the window, "Drop your guns or I'll shoot you!"

Julian heard a barking dog.

Emilio grabbed Victor and yelled, "If you come closer, I'll shoot him!" To Alfonzo who stood next to him, also still armed, he asked, "Where is the boy? Fetch him!"

Alfonzo looked around the corner wall just in time to see Julian jumping off the porch, and Manuel draping an arm around his shoulders.

"Stop!" he shrieked in a high pitch voice and raised his gun.

At that moment, several police officers pumped Alfonzo with lead.

Julian hugged Manuel, feeling as if he really had a father after all. But, then he turned to watch the house, worried about Victor.

The handler loosed the dog and gave a command to the dog.

The dog ran in and grabbed Emilio by the arm, pulling him to the ground.

Victor, who was much larger than Emilio, and no longer worried about Julian, wrestled the gun from Emilio.

Emilio lay face down on the living room floor, screaming, "Stop this fucking dog!"

A policemen called the dog off and cuffed Emilio.

Diego announced that Alfonzo was dead.

Victor walked outside and grinning weakly at Manuel, raised his arms and shouted, "Glad you came to see us in our moment of victory!"

Then he fainted.

Chapter 25 Doors and Bars

At the station in Guadalajara, a few whacks with a nightstick across Emilio's fingers on a metal table loosened him up for talking with the policemen. Behind his glasses, Emilio's eyes were squeezed shut, as he tried not to grimace.

"Who else were you working with?" Whack! "Why were you taking a boy and a man out of town against their will?"

"I didn't! It was Alfonzo – the one the police killed!"

"Why were you with them? Who put you up to this? Answer me!"

"No one!"

"Really?" The police leaned on Emilio's hand, pressing down with his stick.

"It was just Alfonzo's stupid joke."

"Very funny. Hey, Carlos, did you hear that? These idiots kidnapped a boy and his uncle for fun! And after a hard day's work at the hospital? Or did you steal the ambulance, too?"

The other officer sneered, and scribbled something in his notes.

The first officer said to Emilio, "I'll break your fingers! Are you sure you don't want to think about this some more? We will go easier on you if you tell us who put you up to it. We have a good idea who it was anyway. Save your own skin! No one else will."

"No! Stop. I tell you!"

The policeman continued to press down.

"It was Dr. Bella, I swear!"

Later that night, in Guadalajara, Carmen Bella was calmly placing her manicured toes on her bathroom's lavender and rose rug. Her bath complete, she reached for her thick towel and dried off daintily, admiring her own good looks in the slightly misty, oversized, floor length mirror. After pulling on a thick, terry cloth robe and combing out her long, black hair, she looked in the mirror again. Apparently satisfied, she left the bathroom. She padded downstairs to her modern kitchen and set a kettle on the stove. She put CD of Mozart on in her country floral living room, and then made a cup of English tea. Everything she had was imported, for she believed all the best things were made elsewhere, by people whom she did not trust, the exception being that their money and their products were good.

She sat down with her tea and a romantic novel, and began to read quietly when someone pounded on the door. Frowning slightly at the rude sounding knock, she went to the door and peeked through the small viewing glass. It was the police.

She opened the door calmly and said an icy voice, "What do you want?"

"Sorry *Doctora*, but we have to bring you down to headquarters for questioning."

"Outrageous! On what possible pretext?"

"There has been a kidnapping from the hospital."

"Talk to the head administrator of the hospital then!"

"You have three minutes to put on some clothes. Your questions will be answered when you talk to the chief."

"How dare you? Tell the chief to come to me and explain this." She began closing the door.

The officer put his foot in the door. Then he shouldered his way in.

"Oh no you don't!" she shrieked. She slapped his face and pushed him away.

He called to his partner, "Help me cuff her. She's not coming in voluntarily."

While Carmen Bella screamed and tried to claw their faces, they cuffed her.

She said coldly, "I'll get you two fired for this. You don't know what you're doing."

At the strangely bright Guadalajara station, Victor waited in the bull pen. After having been separated from his companions, transported over a rugged terrain – a ride two hours long – and questioned for an hour, he was still not allowed to leave.

Emilio was at the same station, in handcuffs, with bandages on his hands.

Meanwhile, Manuel was in the Puerto Vallarta hospital, listening to a bandaged Julian talk to his distraught mother.

Julian was pale as he explained to them what had happened. His mother held Julian and cried. Manuel stood near the cross over Julian's hospital bed.

Back at the station, when Dr. Bella was forcefully escorted into the bull pen, she was quiet, her face a frozen mask with black, staring eyes. Victor gaped at her tousled appearance, the bathrobe, and the handcuffs, feeling gratified. Victor knew he wasn't looking well himself. He rubbed his stubble-covered jaw with roughened, dirty hands. He tiredly watched the Guadalajara police chief, Trujillo, promptly end a hushed discussion with his officers. Victor wondered if he would put any of this in his paper – it was interesting. Maybe some version of it at least, he decided – later, much later.

He was about to ask when he could go home and take a shower, but then he overheard Dr. Bella answering Chief Trujillo, "He's a liar if he said that. I don't believe it. This is ridiculous! What do you really want, money?"

Victor watched the chief spread his hands, placatingly. Then, as if he hadn't heard her offer, he said, "Now Carmen, don't take it so badly. I just have to ask you some questions. It's about some home surgeries. A boy who says he didn't need his eye removed. He was kidnapped in an ambulance by a couple of your employees."

"I want to call my lawyer. Now! Let me have the telephone."

"Of course." As he stepped over to the other bulky desk to bring an extension to her, Dr. Bella spied Victor, who smiled. It was habit; he always smiled at women.

"What are you smiling at and why are you here?!" she demanded.

"I refuse to stay in the same room with that man," She shouted. "He is a phony and a liar!"

The chief jerked his head toward the door, staring meaningfully at a desk clerk. The clerk cleared his throat, "Eh, Victor. You can stay at this hotel, La Playa. *Pero*, you cannot go home. *¿Entiende?* Stay nearby," and handed Victor a card with directions to the hotel.

As Victor walked, he thought, "*My girlfriend won't understand this.* He sighed. *What a pity. But damn, it's good to be alive!*

Even during his first calling, illegally importing goods, which involved selling to criminals, and crossing the border illegally, he hadn't been this close to death.

The next day, Victor endured yet another interview. However, this one was in the comparatively posh offices of the Ministry of Health. "So right after you saw Dr. Bella, you were abducted in the stairwell?"

"Yes. Once again. It was right after."

"Had you seen them before, the men who abducted you?" an investigator for the ministry of health inquired, writing these answers down as if he were hearing them for the first time.

"No, I hadn't seen them, but Julian said he had seen one of the men, Emilio, around the clinic in Puerto Vallarta."

The investigator looked up, "Are you sure he said this?"

"Why you don't ask him? He's healthy, right??"

"Yes. Be calm."

"I have to get back to my newspaper!"

The minister tapped his pen on his pad, quite bored with these protestations. "Just a few more questions and then you may take a break, Señor. You have to stick around."

"*¡Increíble!*" Victor shouted, and he stalked out of the room, looking for a cigarette, although normally, he only smoked an occasional cigar.

Back in Puerto Vallarta, Julian left the Puerto Vallarta hospital with stitches in his arm, an immobilizing sling, and antibiotics. Fortunately, the bullet had missed his bone.

Additional security now patrolled the Guadalajara hospital. Now hospital administration prohibited doctors from making any home visits or after-hours appointments.

Mexico City's police chief had stepped down earlier that year, 1998, after fighting unsuccessfully for nine months to stem a wave of kidnappings, robberies and slayings there. The mood of the people everywhere, including the nearby Jalisco province, was insistent: clean up on crime. For a change, authorities in Puerto Vallarta and Guadalajara were taking a kidnapping case seriously.

Victor was bored after visiting the Ministry of Health, so he called Manuel to ask what was going on. He was looking for news, not another job to do. He got one anyway.

He leaned out the window to watch the sunny streets while he spoke, "Audrey! *¿Como estás?* No, I'm still here. Is Manuel around?"

"No, he's at the factory," she said, a bit irritably, Victor thought, and he wondered what was bothering her. Manuel couldn't have been home long, yet he was already at work. He wondered if he would do the same if he had a lovely little wife. Probably, since like Manuel, he ran his own business, and one's business cannot run for long without the boss's attention.

"May I call him there?"

Audrey was packing to go to the resort. Her stomach was bothering her. Sometimes the water in Mexico gave her digestive problems. She often drank bottled, but didn't feel it was necessary to do so all of the time. "Certainly, 515-0091. Are you doing any investigating of your own, Victor?"

"No. All I do is answer questions," Victor said.

Audrey laughed.

"Do you have any sisters in the United States that you could introduce me to?" he asked.

Audrey laughed again, a musical sound, "I have one, but she just got married."

"Oh, if only I had asked you sooner. Well, I will see what Manuel is doing now, *sí?*"

When Victor hung up, he leaned back against the cool, white stucco window frame; its thick walls comforted him. It was a beautiful day, and it was wonderful to be safe again.

He dialed again, and waited for the operator to connect him.

"Manuel's Rosewood Company."

"Manuel, it's Victor. How are you and Julian?"

"The boy is okay. He was stitched up last night, and he's home with his mother today. I'm fine. Are you still butting heads with the police and the Ministry of Health?"

"I am butting heads with buttheads of all types. I saw Dr. Bella last night at the police station. She recognized me and started screaming."

"Then what happened?"

"Perhaps I should be grateful to her, since they finally let me go, so she'd calm down. Hah! I got some rest at a hotel. Why aren't you home with the *mamacita*? She sounds lonely to me."

"You know it has been too long since I looked after my business."

"Is the lumber company doing poorly?"

Victor could hear the whining of the saws and an unaccustomed hardness to Manuel's voice. Manuel said, "Not as poorly as the marriage, apparently. Audrey seems to think Julian getting hurt is all my fault. His mom, Marisol, was hysterical. We are responsible for what happened to Julian, you know."

Victor hung his head and closed his eyes against the white sun reflecting off of everything. His gut wrenched as he thought of Julian almost getting raped. That was worse than being shot in the arm. He wondered if Julian had told his mother about that. He said, "I gotta find people who know that shrew doctor. Any ideas?"

"I met a couple that saw her after hours. An American couple, Nadía... Nadía and David. The lady received new corneas after hours. They weren't much help, but maybe now…. Check the La Tapatía hotel."

"Does Marisol blame me?"

"I don't think so. I think she and my wife both hold me solely responsible."

"But I am guilty too."

"Things didn't work out the way we wanted, did they? I'm sorry, Victor."

After he hung up, Victor imagined how terrified Marisol must have been. *We could have lost Julian.* Victor hadn't been close to his own family. Nor had he experienced deep feelings before. Now his heart tormented him with guilt, love, and anger at himself.

He strolled down to a local café for a bit of café au lait, and some croissants, breathing deeply, trying to lift his spirits. There were plenty of tourists. One of them would know where La Tapatía was. He started asking, and someone told him, while staring at him as if he were *loco*. He looked down and realized with a start that his pants were torn and dirty, and he needed a haircut. He had forgotten to fully groom himself for the first time since he stopped working with coyotes, drug dealers, and thieves. Deciding to go to a barber and then buy some new pants, he left without reading the newspaper, a first for him. Victor decided to look like a gentleman before he tried to talk to the Americans, even if he spent all of the cash he had left.

Cleaned up by the afternoon, he walked into the lobby of the La Tapatía, its graceful, arching walls were covered with hand painted flowers. He asked the young clerk for the room number of a David and Nadia.

"Do you know the last names?" the clerk asked helpfully.

"Oh, no, we were just going to meet for a drink."

"Oh, *sí*. Well, a David and Nadia Flores just checked out. But I think they are in the bar."

Victor wandered over to the nearby bar. About twenty people, many of them looking American, sat around the palm leaf-covered bar overlooking the pool. A separate section of the bar extended into the tree-lined pool past the huge sliding glass doors. Victor sat down and ordered a Corona and lime. As he sat sipping the beer, he looked around, wondering what to do.

Some men were playing cards at their table, and calling each other very insulting names in a playful way. There was a couple that dressed alike; both the lady and the man wore khaki pants and a striped shirt. Victor disapproved of this, feeling that a lady should look like a woman, and the more so, the better.

"Everything is so beautiful!" a lady across the bar was saying in an overly loud voice. She was cheaply dressed, flashy, a woman that turns heads, and many men besides Victor were looking her over. A blond man sitting near her was speaking quietly to her, and she nodded, adding, "Well, since doctor Bella won't see me, I told them, 'If you won't let me see Dr. Bella, then I don't want to see any of your damn doctors.'"

"It doesn't matter now," the man said, lighting a cigarette.

Victor knew he had to introduce himself – quickly.

"Bartender, please serve those two people one more of whatever they are drinking," he said to the man who had served him his beer.

The bartender nodded and made two margaritas.

"These are from the gentleman over there," the bartender said as he served the drinks.

The lady and her man looked over at him, expecting to see an old friend perhaps, or an acquaintance among the expatriates of America who sit around spending their retirement funds and disability checks.

Victor wondered briefly if he should try the direct approach, and decided not to. "You are leaving Guadalajara? Don't you like it here?"

"Have we met?" the blond man asked, blowing smoke in Victor's face.

"Please excuse me, my name is Victor, and I couldn't help but overhear that the hospital wouldn't let you make an appointment to see Dr. Bella?"

The woman leaned forward. She said, "My name is Nadia and this is David, my fiancé," putting out her hand, and flashing a flirtatious smile.

Victor kissed her hand; then said the formalities to David, who leaned back and sipped the drink Victor had bought him.

"Do you know where she is?" Nadia chattered on without waiting for a reply, "I had an appointment with her, but she never arrived. I waited and waited, while the nurse kept paging her and calling the hospital administrators to see if she had called. I wasn't sure if the doctor was being forgetful, rude, or if something serious had happened to her. She has helped me so much. She seems like a lady who gets things done – not like someone who just doesn't show up."

Victor nodded, and sat down in a nearby bar stool as soon as someone got up. The seat was still warm.

David lowered his margarita. "Do you know the doctor?" He asked.

Victor smiled his winning smile, "Yes, I do! She is, as you say, someone who gets things done. I saw her, very recently, but she was upset at the time."

Nadia asked, "About what?"

"I'm not sure. You see, the police had just rescued me from a nasty traffic accident, a hit and run, so I was there answering questions and filling out a report when she arrived. She was arguing with the officer who was dragging her in. She was cuffed actually, and in her bathrobe." He watched the couple exchange looks, alarm registering on their faces. He continued talking as if he hadn't noticed, "I was outraged; she is the eye specialist for the entire area, yet the police treated her like a common criminal. I couldn't say anything at the time. The police were helping me. And if you get them angry? Well, they aren't helpful."

Both Nadia and David suddenly seemed preoccupied with the salt on their glasses.

Victor continued, "I wonder if any of her patients will come to her defense, or if they're all too poor, or busy making money. She has operated on so many children in the mountains around here who could never afford to pay her. Did you know that? It seems a shame." He slumped over the bar, appearing to brood while gazing at his glass.

"She is the nicest doctor," Nadia said. "I would feel awful if she didn't find justice. I mean, after she helped all those children... And me – I can see for the first time in years!"

David concentrated, stabbing at his ice cubes. He looked up earnestly, "You know, maybe we should see what this is about before we leave."

CHAPTER 26 JULIAN'S QUEST

"It's a summons to court, Señora, in Guadalajara. You and your son, Julian, must testify in a court of law."

"But it's September and the boys just started back in school. I can't leave my job, and who will take care of Enrique?"

Julian listened to his mother talk to the court appointed bad news messenger. The court date would be sometime next month.

Julian tried to look nonchalant, leaning against the wall, his injured right arm curled on his chest. He pretended to read the book that he awkwardly held with his left hand. Meanwhile, Enrique colored in a coloring book on the floor.

Julian hadn't watched television since Manuel had taken it away. He'd actually gotten used to reading, and had learned to like it. Suddenly, Julian couldn't pretend to ignore what came next.

"You have no choice." The man in a suit said sternly, "The *Corte Suprema* requires you to come. You will be provided with living quarters and meals during the case."

"That is not enough!" his mother shouted, "Who will pay the rent? Who will guarantee that I have a job when I return?"

"Señora, I'm sorry," the man said, but he did not sound sorry as he firmly slapped the summons into his mother's hand. Then he turned and strode toward his big car.

She slammed the warped wooden door and whirled around, "Not enough evidence? Can't they see that our lives have been ruined enough? We have told them everything already!"

Julian stared after her as she turned on her heels into the kitchen. Soon, he heard the sound of pans and cans of what he knew to be chicken and enchilada sauce, being thumped on the chipped, tile counter. Julian brooded, nodding blankly as his brother held his coloring page of a burro up for his approval.

"It's nice, 'rique."

His brother's big brown and green eyes looked sad.

Julian said to him, loudly enough for his mother to hear, "Don't worry Pancho, I won't let the mean man bother Mom anymore. If he comes back, we'll shoot him with your slingshot. Do you have your artillery? No? You better get it ready!"

Enrique happily got supplies ready in case the "mean man" came back. Meanwhile, Julian pondered his mother's problems. She was proud and would not ask for help, if there was any possible way to avoid that, so he went over in his mind the people who had the means to help them: Javier and Adelia Neri, Manuel and Audrey, Alan and Lena Todd.

His mother said that they needed rent paid while they were in court. How long would a court case last? Alan and Lena would probably take care of that, if he asked them. They needed someone to take care of Enrique and take him to school. Audrey could take care of that, he felt sure. His mother was worried about having a job when she returned, so maybe if she lost her job, the Neri's could hire her to cook and clean. But they already had maids.... Adelia would surely be willing to help his mother find a job. His stomach churned with renewed guilt.

The gun that he had stolen from the Neri's after they had hired him – trusted him – seemed to have left a burning sensation in his hand. Fear crept over him when he worried if it would come out in the trial that he had stolen the gun from them. He dreaded the shame that he would bring to his mother.

He was brought back to the present by his mother's call to dinner and the aroma of chicken enchiladas.

"I'm coming Mom," he called. "Come on Enrique, you heard Mom. Leave the artillery there by the window."

Few things dampened Julian's appetite, and he ate heartily, "These are great, the best. Can I have some more?"

"*Sí, hijo.* They are the same as always," she insisted, but the corners of her mouth turned up a little.

Julian wanted his mother to stay cheerful when dinner was over. "Mom, I will do the dishes tonight. You relax. I mean," he stared stupidly at his arm, "Enrique and I will wash dishes, won't we?"

The little boy nodded brightly, eager to be of help.

Now tears trailed down his mother's cheeks. Julian stood frozen for a moment, dreading a gale of sobs. Marisol stood up. She looked frail and tired. She came over to Julian, and wrapped her arms around him, "*Tú eres un buen hijo*. So, we will be all right no matter what, *sí?*"

She smelled good, and her embrace was comforting. When she went to the living room to rest as he had ordered her to do, he scoured the pans awkwardly while Enrique held them and rinsed. Meanwhile, he made plans to enlist the help of his family, and family friends.

The next day, after school, he walked up the road to Manuel and Melissa's house with Ricky. Ricky said, "I'll help you get caught up in school. Don't worry, you can copy all of my papers – I save all of them, just in case." He grinned at Julian, then jumped up to grab a tree branch and hang from it, swinging for a few beats.

Julian doubted that this would be enough. How would he understand anything to pass the tests?

But it was worth a try. Anything to avoid being left behind to repeat a grade in secondary school while his friends moved on. Anyway, he knew he had to pass, because *Bigotes* might get angry and cut off the money that he sends to his mother.

"What's the matter?" Ricky asked.

Feeling the building heat of the afternoon during the uphill climb to Ricky's home, and not wanting to answer that, Julian said, "Why isn't Esther in school with us anymore?"

"Didn't you hear? She's going to have a baby. She has to get married."

"Huh? I … guess that's great."

"Not really. My mom says it's going to ruin her life," Ricky said as he kicked a rock.

"How could she – you know? Her papa is so strict and she's so *good*."

"Well, her boyfriend wasn't interested in her being *good*. He's about twenty and her dad probably feels like he's a good match anyway since he's rich."

Julian suddenly wanted to be rich too, but not as rich as Javier; that would invite trouble. He envied both the boyfriend and Esther, even if she was ruining her life like Ricky's mom said. What if the man left her, like María's father did to Rosa, or died and left her to care for the child alone, like his own father did to his mother? Julian stopped in the road, it was odd timing, but "ruining her life" brought his own mother's situation back to him.

"Do you think your mom would watch Enrique for us for a while?"

"How long?"

"I don't know," Julian said, shrugging. He regretted it instantly and cradled his aching, injured arm.

"Well, it doesn't matter, anyway. She'll do it," Ricky said lightly as he bounded up the narrow stairs nestled in a cluster of banana trees that led to his house.

Julian trudged up afterwards. In his mind, he tried out a few phrases since, *Would you please take care of my little brother for about a month?* just wasn't going to be easy to say. Is there any other way to ask besides just coming out with it? He wondered.

They went into the kitchen and started harvesting all of the edible contents out of the refrigerator.

"Where is your mom?" Julian asked.

"Oh, she's probably in her office, writing," Ricky said as he chewed on a cold piece of roast beef, "Don't you want to catch up on some school work first?"

"Uh, would you mind if I ask her right now? I just really need to know."

"Sure! C'mon."

Ricky led the way through the wide open doors that into a large, verdant courtyard. At the far end was small cabin. Ricky walked up to the window, "Mom?"

"Hmm?"

"Um, Julian wants to ask you something."

Audrey peeked out of the window, then she came out into the sunlight, squinting her light blue eyes against the tropical sun which hit her face directly. She looked tired, and older than Julian remembered.

"Mrs. Romero, uh, some man came over our house yesterday and said that me and her have to go to Guadalajara for a trial. She's really worried about it."

Julian tried to lean casually against a wooden chair, but the chair moved. Audrey's mouth twitched in amusement. Ricky studied his tennis shoes as if he'd never noticed how wonderfully fashioned they were until now.

"I knew that you and your mom would have to go. Manuel has to go too. It's a terrible hardship on your mother, isn't it?"

Julian nodded with a manly frown.

"Don't worry. I'll watch Enrique and take him to school when I take Ricky. My Dad and Mom will keep the house paid for while you both are gone. Your mom will have a job when she gets back, if she needs it. I'll hire her at the resort, or if she doesn't want to go that far, I'll help her find a job around here." She laughed and gave him a little hug.

Julian winced at the pain in his arm. Ricky rolled his eyes at Julian, but smiled at his mom.

Audrey teased, "You are quite worrier aren't you? You've got us to help you, and don't ever forget that, okay?"

216

Julian felt his eyes stinging and wet. He bit his lip.

As if she had known what else could possibly be bothering him, she added, "Manuel will take you and your mother up there, so don't worry about that either! You guys go do your homework and then shoot some aliens on the video game or something. Lighten up! Shoo!"

Ricky let Julian copy some of his work, but most of it he forced Julian to prove that he understood it first. Julian felt it was taking him too long this way and said so.

"If you're going to keep up with the class, you better understand what you missed," Ricky insisted, "Especially since you're going away again. I don't want you to be in the lower grade next year. Then we won't have any classes together. You have to study harder."

So, contrary to Audrey's instructions, they did not play Nintendo. Instead, they studied until dinnertime. Ricky invited Julian to stay for dinner, and so both mothers were given the studying explanation, Julian's over the phone.

Manuel joined them for dinner. When he saw Julian, he said, "How's the sharp shooter?"

Julian felt the blood drain out of his face. He was speechless.

Audrey demanded. "What are you talking about?"

"I'm sorry, Julian. That was in poor taste. Can we tell her?"

Julian nodded.

Manuel explained, "Julian here protected himself against rape. When he shot that big idiot in the ambulance, he surprised the Hell out of Victor!"

Manuel said, "Self defense should go over pretty well at the trial. C'mon, Audrey. Don't worry."

"Don't worry that Julian almost.... Don't worry about him shooting a gun?!"

"Look, I'm really sorry about all that. But look at Julian. He's almost a man now. And he's fine. Uh, mostly."

"You damn, macho jerk!"

He grabbed her wrist and pulled her to him. While giving him a reproachful look, Audrey smiled and pulled on his thick black mane. They kissed intimately.

Julian, with his mouth hanging open, looked at Ricky. Ricky grinned at him and shrugged. If Julian's mother and father had been so affectionate, that had been hidden from him. He realized, for the first time in his life, that his own mother was a lonely woman. It had been nine years. He vowed to himself that no matter what, he would finish school, and get a good job. The first thing he would do would be to give his mother a vacation.

During the plain and delicious meal of chicken, potatoes, cornbread, cauliflower and beans, Julian analyzed Manuel's appearance between second and third helpings. He said, "Manuel, you got more gray hair when Victor and I were kidnapped. You must've been worried about us."

"You don't even know the half of it," Manuel said, glancing at his wife.

Ricky laughed. Then he went back to scraping his dish to get the last of his dinner.

Audrey said to Manuel. "The silver hair only makes you more handsome." Then she got up to wash the dishes.

Julian and Ricky resumed studying after dinner until dark. Then and Manuel drove Julian home.

Manuel drove extra slowly, as if he wasn't concentrating solely on the drive through the dark, rutted scars on the earth between rows of adobe homes and shacks where there were no streetlights at all. He said, "Julian?"

"Yeah?"

"They've asked María and her mother to testify too. I want you to go with my son tomorrow and invite them to ride with us to Guadalajara. I don't want them to take a bus, and they don't have a phone. I would go with you, but I need to put in some extra hours tomorrow."

"No problem!"

His response was automatic; he would do anything Manuel asked. They pulled up to Julian's home in silence.

His mother and Enrique were already asleep. He wondered how María would feel about having to go to the trial. After all, Dr. Bella had robbed her of her sight. He felt anxious about seeing her tomorrow as he had very confused feelings and had difficulty falling asleep. He was attracted to her, yet he was frightened by her blindness; maybe more than most guys would be, since he was halfway blind.

CHAPTER 27
PREPARING FOR THE INQUEST

Julian rode in the middle seat of Manuel's van next to María and her mother. Rosa, who passed around baked goodies and bottles of cold lemonade. This earned much appreciation from Julian, who was always hungry. However, he kept running out of things to say to María.

Now and then during the ride to Guadalajara, he tried to smile at María, but remembered that she wouldn't see him. Then he would start to point out a view of the jungles, or an orchard, or a funny dog in boy's wagon by the side of the road, and the words froze in his throat.

In front of him, his mother sat, speaking with Manuel about *el presidente* Zedillo, the prices of various foods, and his own progress, or lack of it, in school. She was wearing a scarf and earrings. She looked younger than she normally did, and she held up her end of the conversation with Manuel. Although his mother couldn't read well, she always asked about the news and helped spread it around too. Occasionally, Manuel would call back a question or comment to one of the riders in the back seat, but the noise from the engine and the road made conversation difficult. Rosa, seated on the other side of María, entered into the conversation occasionally, but mostly, she just smiled and nodded. She seemed worn out; old even, like a grandmother. Julian wondered why her husband had left her to raise María by herself. When she smiled at him, he looked away, afraid she would read his thoughts somehow. It was confusing trying to understand why some grownups didn't stay and raise their children. Ricky had once insisted that Julian's father hadn't intentionally committed suicide by starving himself during his depression, so he couldn't be faulted for leaving Julian. *At least I knew my father,* he thought.

María seemed to gaze out the window or at her hands, listening to everything, but remaining silent. She was radiantly beautiful; her long, black hair was pulled back from her face with a series of small-beaded combs.

She broke the silence between them, "Are you nervous about going to court?"

"Yeah, I am. But, it can't be as bad as what we already went through with her."

"She's done her worst – to us, but I wonder what she is doing now?"

"Victor said they called her into court for questioning, so she's probably not doing much. Now they want to question us."

At the mention of Victor, Marisol turned to listen.

"How can we prove anything?"

Julian said, "Just tell the truth I guess, and hope that it's enough to stop her from ever doing bad things to other kids."

"Those guys who hurt you have to be punished, too."

Julian suddenly remembered what that large man, Raúl, had tried to do to him. María must never know about that. Then he remembered the gun pointed at him by Emilio, and the men's laughter as they spoke about burying him in the dirt. He remembered the shovel lying incongruously in the corner of the ambulance.

María touched his shoulder softly, "Are you all right?"

"I was just remembering some of the bad things that happened when they abducted Victor and me," Julian confided.

"Well, like you said, we just have to tell them the whole truth, then you can forget about it."

Julian smiled wryly, "Yeah, you're right again."

At the end of the hot, two-hour drive, they pulled up in front of a white, Spanish style hotel with orange tile roofing, white arches, and a small courtyard with a fountain in the front. Beneath the arches in cool shade, some green wicker chairs were arranged near a water cooler, and potted plants were placed neatly all around.

Julian couldn't wait to get out of the van, and when he did, he ran to the water cooler and drank a few paper cups full. He remembered his manners just in time to fill a cup for María, who was being led up the walkway by her mother. He put the cup into her hand, and poured another for Rosa, who smiled at him kindly. Julian chided himself for not thinking of María's needs earlier. *It's not right that the only person who helps her is her mother*, he thought.

"So we're all here! *¡Bienvenido!*" Victor called out, as he strode out of the office toward them looking as cool as ice cream in his white silk shirt and pants.

Manuel met him and the two embraced. They looked about as opposite as could be; Manuel was dressed in black, and was as hot, sweaty, and shaggy as Victor was cool and groomed.

"*Como estás,* Victor?" Manuel asked. "It looks like you're being treated well."

"They treat you as well as you make them treat you."

"Point well taken."

The two women stood near the water cooler watching the men, unsure what to do next. María waited near them. Rosa was dressed in the baggy garb of a widowed peasant, a dark purple dress. Marisol was dressed surprisingly well, in her cheap but well-fitting slacks, heels and polyester knit blouse.

Victor addressed them all, "Don't worry about your rooms – that's all taken care of thanks to the graciousness of our governor. Your suites are near mine on the second floor – Ah... *Hola-*"

Victor looked at Marisol, "I'm really sorry about this," he said.

Marisol smiled politely.

Julian knew only too well why his mother wasn't fond of Victor, for he'd listened to his mother's harangues about the jeopardy Victor had put Julian in. She laid all the blame at his feet.

Manuel misunderstood the awkward pause and thought Victor couldn't recall her name, so he supplied the names afresh.

Victor regained his equanimity and greeted Julian, "¡*Hombre!*" He grabbed him by the hand and pulled him close for a bear hug. The familiar crushing of his older friend's strong arms focused Julian's mind, as if he suddenly stopped watching the scene from above his body, and began to feel emotions again.

Victor said, "How was your trip?"

Julian answered, "Well, it wasn't too boring."

"Of course not, with your lovely friend to talk to."

Manuel coughed and said, "Take us to our rooms, Victor."

"*Sí, claro.*" Victor said, "Let me take your bags, Señoras," and he hauled the women's bags out of the rear seat, hoisted them all on his shoulder like a burro loaded down for the marketplace, and led the way up through the warm lobby.

Even with the ceiling fans on and the windows always open, it was too hot upstairs to unpack. The wilted, damp group congregated again at the courtyard, cooled somewhat by the spray of the fountain. They watched Victor expectantly, but he seemed content to relax. Julian kicked the cement wall of the fountain.

At last, Manuel spoke, "Have you been told when we are expected to be in court?"

"*Sí*, 8 tomorrow."

"What's going to happen first?" Julian asked Manuel. "Do I have to talk in court tomorrow?"

María and her mother were biting their lips, frowning, looking like mirror images of one another. Marisol awkwardly put a comforting arm around her tall son. Julian blushed a little, but he stayed close.

Victor answered, "*Sí*, they will be asking more questions. Would anyone like to get a drink and then take an early look at the courthouse?"

After walking for awhile, the two mothers purchased some necessities at a nearby pharmacy while the others drank their *aguas frescas*, and read the headlines of the magazines and newspapers posted all about a large, sidewalk newsstand. Julian read the comics on the front table to María while the old newsman inside watched them. Victor bought *El Occidental*, while exchanging friendly words with the newsman on the state of business.

"How's the business here in front of the police station?" he asked. "Do you get many police buying papers?" he asked.

"Business is good, but not many police buy the newspaper," the man answered.

"Maybe they already know the news well enough from making arrests and watching the town. What do you think?"

"Could be, or perhaps they don't want to see themselves in the photographs."

There was a photo of police in riot gear chasing families out of their shantytowns on the front page.

"I'll bet you are right." Victor smiled. "That picture is downright unflattering."

He paid the old newsman two centavos. Another article on the front page said, "*Cientos Esperan Trasplante*" ("Hundreds Wait for Transplants"). He read the article then, grim-faced, and handed Manuel the paper. Manuel read carefully. He exchanged glances with Victor. Manuel finished the article while slumping against narrow strip of pharmacy wall between two huge windows. He learned that in that year, 1998, in their state, Jalisco, there had only been forty-nine cadaver donations. There were thirty-six recorded cornea transplants, yet, 350 people were on a waiting list for corneas. The situation was worse for other body parts, such as kidneys, for which 1,500 people were listed as waiting.

Julian scanned the headlines rapidly, and saw the grim faces of his uncles, as he now thought of them.

Then his mother burst out of store, and angrily told Manuel, "I saw Dr. Bella's name on several medicines in the pharmacy! She has a brand of eye drops, vitamins, and some pills. Come see!"

Rosa, who had followed Marisol, nodded in agreement, bewildered.

They went inside, and Victor and Manuel read every side of each box. There was, sure enough, Dr. Bella's Bright Eyes drops, Dr. Bella's Bright Eyes vitamins A and E, "To restore clear night vision," and Dr. Bella's Bright Eyes brand alertness pills. Every package had Dr. Bella's picture on it.

The stunned group practically backed out of the pharmacy.

Rosa laid her hand imploringly on Marisol's arm and asked, "What chance do we have in court if she sells her medicines right across the street from the police station?"

Victor and Manuel had known that she sold medicines, but somehow seeing them made Dr. Bella even more formidable.

Victor said jauntily, "Well, the police simply don't know yet how worthless her medicines are, because they don't understand that a great number of her patients wouldn't even use them – because after she is done operating, they have no eyes to use them on! Come on, let's go see the courthouse."

They glumly followed, each one frowning, and looking away from María.

Somehow, María seemed to sense the tension, but she cheerfully asked questions about what they were passing. The group strolled past progressively more ancient buildings lining a teaming, exhaust-choked boulevard of the city's center. Julian soon became distracted by the busy city and cheered by María's enthusiasm.

Eventually, everyone relaxed and began to talk of other things. They enjoyed commenting on the crowds, the buildings, signs, and the statues representing revolutionaries in front of a huge park.

The later in the afternoon it became, the more the city woke up from its drowsy, sun-induced rest. Everywhere now, people were strolling with what seemed to be their entire families in tow, including numerous babies in carriages and strollers. Young couples in love, with or without little babies, seemed to be everywhere, getting in taxis, or sitting on benches. The excitement of the city was a new experience for Julian and he rather liked it.

Julian instinctively began to guide María. It felt strange and wonderful to hold her arm, as he'd never touched a girl before, except once when a girl at primary school impulsively hugged him upon their graduation. Esther had held María's arm when they went to a movie after María got her prosthetic eyes. Up until the day they watched movies together, the only girl who had ever interested him was the mysterious and intelligent Esther. They began discussing Esther's upcoming wedding as they passed a gazebo.

"I wonder if she really loves him?" María said.

"Why wouldn't she?" Julian asked, looking away from her large bosom, even though María wouldn't have known, he chided himself. *She's grown a lot recently*, he thought, smiling.

"Well, I couldn't love him. I don't like how quiet he is. I could hardly tell he was there when we had lunch at Esther's parents' house. When he does say something, it's always serious things about politics, like how Zedillo is the best man to run for the PRI party. I mean, that's important, but then he goes on and on. He's so boring that everybody at the table in the backyard patio was falling asleep. It became so quiet except for his voice and the snoring of the dogs, under the table. Even the chickens stopped clucking. They fell asleep by the snoring dogs by my feet."

Julian laughed, but he wondered if he was boring too. He said, "Esther's pretty serious, so maybe they're well matched."

"Yeah, maybe they are. Esther talks endlessly about being pregnant and about being a mother. She sounds like the diaper commercials on TV."

Ahead of them, the adults stopped to observe the courthouse that butted unceremoniously up to the sidewalk. They hurried up to join the adults and stopped.

"Why are we stopping?" María asked.

Julian said, "It's the courthouse. It's big and important looking – like a president lives there or something."

"*¡Es nada!*" Victor said, curling his lip in distaste. "Across the street is the opera house. *That* is beautiful. Let's show these country cousins what the city holds, ay?" He lifted his chin to Manuel questioningly. "This evening is the perfect time for a stroll! You will see the cathedrals and the monuments to our great philosophers, artists and politicians, and in the plaza, we will be diverted from our troubles by the flutes of our indigenous peoples."

The women oohed and aahed, "*¿Sí? ¿De veras? ¡Qué bueno!*"

Manuel addressed the group; "It's good for us to enjoy ourselves tonight, for tomorrow it begins. We will see if there is justice to be had in Mexico."

CHAPTER 28 THE TRIAL BEGINS

"This is stupid!" Julian complained, when, for the fifth time, the lawyer said that she would be with them in a moment. His group huddled together on one of the many crowded benches lining the long, tiled hall which resounded with the hurried footsteps of lawyers, clerks, and police walked past, followed by a few frightened looking families, angry young men with baseball or cowboy hats pulled down over their heads. A runt mongrel at the end of a makeshift leather thong trotted by, his toenails clicking. They'd waited two hours. The men had read every last article in that morning's *The Occidental*, which they had again bought at the newspaper stand in front of the pharmacy.

The adults allowed María and Julian to walk across the street and buy a balloon on a stick and sodas for everyone, but the novelty of the buying spree soon wore off. They all were hungry, so Julian's mother passed out the sweet bread she always brought, a habit from when he and Enrique were little. Julian was chewing on a fluffy, pink roll. At last, Mrs. Sepulveda, the lawyer, came, her heels clicking on the tile.

She pulled Manuel aside and told him in quiet tones, "The customers you met coming out of the hospital, David and Nadia Flores, have not returned any of my calls or letters to their residence in San Diego, so we haven't got any corroboration of your testimony from them. I'm sorry."

Manuel nodded pensively. "Can you subpoena them or something?"

"Maybe, if you have others who can confirm your stories." She glanced at the group that sat watching them. "Brought your witnesses?"

"Yes, the friends I told you about who know something about Dr. Bella."

"Good." She looked the group over again and smiled. "Well, all right then. I'd like to start with Julian. Ready, Julian?"

He rose and took off his baseball cap. She led him to a separate room for what Julian hoped would be his interview about this case.

Julian quickly swallowed his last bite of bread and nervously eyed his lawyer, who sat across from him at a large, gray table in one of the black chairs. Mrs. Sepulveda, from Mexico City, was a nice-looking woman in a red and black suit. She had been gentle and friendly with him the last time they had met in Puerto Vallarta, during and after his hospital stay.

She leaned forward. "Tell me the truth. Julian, why did you go back to the hospital the last time?"

Julian responded as if he'd been caught cheating at school, as he'd done once to get a glass of punch. He still felt humiliated by the memory, for the other students had teased him.

"We wanted Dr. Bella to make the same mistake again, to say I needed surgery," he said, hunching over.

"Did she?"

"No, a nurse sent me to get eyedrops, but then the elevator was closed off. I told Victor, 'If we want to leave anytime soon, we had better go down the stairs.' At the second story, near the ambulance entrance, we were attacked and thrown inside an ambulance, and then they drove us a long way away …well, you know the rest."

Mrs. Sepulveda made some notes then frowned at him. "Was Doctor Bella directing the kidnappers, or did they mention her?"

"No." A sinking feeling took hold of Julian.

"Have you told me everything about how you got the gun and why you shot Raúl?"

"Yes! Why do you keep asking me that?" *Maybe she's decided that she is going to turn me in for stealing the gun*, he worried.

"Have you ever had any other homosexual experiences?"

"No! I told you that before!" He stood up, ready to bolt from the room, wild-eyed, his long hair matted and sweaty where his baseball cap had been.

Señora Sepulveda's small frame carried a voice as commanding as any man's. "Sit down, Julian! I have to ask these questions. I read the affidavit from the American doctor who said your eyes were clear when he saw you. Some of the Centro Medico's doctors have suggested that it's possible your cornea healed while you were en route to the U.S."

Julian was no longer in the mood to converse. "So? Why'd she want to remove my eye then, if it was going to heal by itself? Why did my Mama find an office full of children missing one or both eyes in the mountain pueblo where I was born? Has anybody at all looked into that yet? No, I'll bet. Not even after Mr. Todd reported everything to the Ministry of Health."

She leaned across the table, her eyes bulging, like his principal's at school.

"Julian, I'm trying to help you," she said.

"Sure you are," he muttered, arms crossed. "Can I leave now?"

She shot a tight-lipped, business smile his way, "Yes, you may go. Ask your friend Victor to come in."

Julian left, slamming the door behind him. His friends and family on the bench looked up at him, startled.

"Victor!" He called.

Victor rose from the bench where he was sitting next to Marisol and walked toward him. When Julian stormed by Victor, he hissed quietly, so the women – especially his mother, wouldn't hear, "The lawyer is in a bitchy mood."

The elder man whistled slowly and whispered, "Calm down, little burro." He gave Julian's shoulder a squeeze.

Victor opened the door grandly, smiled at the lawyer and said, "How's the lady tiger today?"

Her head snapped up from her notes. "I'm fine," she said icily, but relented upon seeing his handsome face grinning at her flirtatiously. "How's the self-employed investigator?"

Victor tilted his head and shrugged. "So so. Could be better, could be worse. What can you do for us? Have you spoken to the judge yet?" He noticed that she had very fine legs.

"Yes. He wants more information." She self-consciously tugged her skirt down. "Sit down, please."

Victor felt the familiar sense of satisfaction in his power over women, smiled again at her, and sat down.

She cleared her throat. "The kidnapping cannot be directly linked to Dr. Bella, yet. Only one of the kidnappers has implicated her, and he may have other motives, such as a lover's quarrel. In addition, several Guadalajara doctors have said that although she may have been mistaken to recommend removal of Julian's eye, no doctor can always correctly predict what cases will clear up, and which will worsen. I don't want to say miracle, but every doctor I've spoken to has seen his share of sudden, unexplained healings. What we need now are the names of other alleged victims in order to establish more factual evidence."

"I brought a girl named María and her mama. They are sitting right outside this door." He pointed to the door lazily. Then he leaned back in the vinyl chair as far as it would allow. "Doctor

Bella removed both of the girl's eyes after she was attacked by a monkey."

Mrs. Sepulveda leaned toward Victor, alert as a little Chihuahua. She repeatedly depressed the button on her retractable ballpoint pen, making an irritating clicking sound. "Do you have any proof that she didn't need her eyes removed?"

"No, but it was done after hours, and Dr. Bella received the cash for the operation, instead of the hospital's cashier."

"Hmmm." She scribbled on her yellow legal pad. "There's probably no record of her surgery if that's the case. Is there anything else that seemed suspicious?'

"Dr. Bella wanted to charge 2,400 pesos for the artificial eyes, an amount that Rosa – that's María's mother – couldn't save in a year. After Julian saved the money he made by working for Javier, Rosa took María to the state hospital here in Guadalajara. Dr. Bella was out of town. A doctor told Rosa they were free, paid for by a government program."

Mrs. Sepulveda said, "Yes. I've heard about that program. Not many people take advantage of it. Please send María and her mother in. I'd like to talk with them now."

"I'd be delighted." Victor stood up languidly. He bowed very slightly. "Is there a place where I could have a cigar?"

"In the courtyard. Just go to the back of the building."

"Thank you Señora." He left the office and walked to the two women whose turn it now was. "María, Señora Rosa. The lawyer is ready for you both to tell her your stories."

Rosa stood up, grabbed her purse, and led María into the office.

Then Victor turned to Marisol and asked her, "Would you mind if I took Manuel out to the courtyard for a smoke? We'll only be a few moments."

Now Julian was left sitting with his mother, who watched Victor's broad, muscular back as he lumbered down the hall with Manuel, who looked tense and nervous like the other men and women in the dingy hall.

Marisol said, "Um um um, that man has such sweet manners, but such bad habits and bad judgment. Trouble, that's what he is."

Julian said, "It's only a cigar, Mom." He slumped down further, played with his cap listlessly and then pulled it down over his head.

Mrs. Sepulveda looked María up and down while making the necessary greetings and even a bit of small talk. María appeared to be an average teenager, dressed as they all were, like the American teens on TV, with a tight, striped, low-cut shirt, dark jeans, and heeled sandals. Only her staring, artificial brown eyes, which made the girl look as if she were in a trance, distinguished her.

The lawyer addressed the mother again, "Señora…"

"Rosa."

"Rosa, would you mind if I asked your daughter some questions?"

"Please, go ahead."

"María, would you please start by describing your injuries after the monkey's attack?"

"Well, I don't know exactly. At first I couldn't believe what had happened. I could see through the blood with one eye, but I couldn't open my other eye. Esther was crying and screaming, 'Help! Look at what that monkey did! Get that monkey away from her!' She scared it away herself. I didn't know she could be that loud."

"You could see through one of your eyes?"

"Yes. Esther's brothers led me to the road and a sympathetic family gave us a ride in their truck to my house, but I could see to get up the stairs leading to the road, and when I climbed in the back of the truck. The truck was blue and gray.

"When I got home, Mama put cold compresses on my eyes and called the hospital for help. I fell asleep. When I woke up, I couldn't open either eye."

"Her eyes were swollen shut tight." Rosa added. The people at the clinic said that Dr. Bella was the eye specialist and she would take good care of María. They said that I was lucky doctor Bella was in town. We don't have insurance or much money. She made us a special deal on the eye extraction, after hours. So, she came to our house, examined her eyes, and then did an emergency operation. There was no nurse, and I had to help. It was horrible." Rosa stifled a sob. She paused to compose herself, and then said, "Afterwards, María could do nothing, and I couldn't afford the prosthetic eyes. For almost a year, María was like a ghost of herself. Then Julian brought money he had saved for the eyes. I couldn't believe it! I had no idea that a fifteen year old boy would do such a thing." The lawyer handed her a tissue. María was listening and twisting a piece of paper in her hands, again and again.

"Your friend Julian tried to do a very good thing," the lawyer said, rocking back in her chair.

Back and forth, María twisted the paper, stroking its feathery softness.

Rosa continued, "Yes. Well, we went to Guadalajara, but Dr. Bella had gone back to Puerto Vallarta, and wasn't expected back right away, so we saw a different doctor. A nice young man."

The lawyer wrote some more notes. Looking up again, she asked, "What was the name of the doctor who said there was some kind of mistake, that the prosthetic eyes were actually free?"

Rosa answered, "Dr. Suarez."

The lawyer put the pen to her mouth and pressed her lips. After a moment she said, "And then what happened?"

"I used the money that Julian gave us to take María to a school for the blind. There were two other patients of Dr. Bella's there." She turned to her daughter, and touched her hand. "Tell her, María,"

"Two other girls, missing both eyes, like me, had been treated by Dr. Bella.

"What are the girl's names?" Mrs. Sepulveda asked.

"Raquel and Vanessa. They are about the same age as I am."

"I need to have their family names and addresses. Without that information, we really can't do anything at all."

"I don't know, but you could call La Escuela Para Los Ciegos; they were there." María said.

Rosa squeezed her daughter's hand. She addressed the lawyer, "There were many more blind patients of Dr. Bella's where Julian's mother, Marisol, went to get Julian's birth certificate, the clinic in the mountain town where he was born. She is waiting in the hallway."

"Oh? Ask Marisol to come in, please."

Rosa hurried to the door and peered around it, "Listen, Marisol. Come here, quickly."

Marisol left her bags with Julian, admonishing him to watch over them, while trying to inconspicuously unstick her dress from the back of her sweating legs. Victor strolled up the hall then and he eyed her shapely legs. Manuel followed him, looking tired.

Marisol stepped into the lawyer's office, smiling shyly. Mrs. Sepulveda said to Marisol, "Please sit down," indicating a fourth chair. "Would you tell me what you saw in the clinic when you went to pick up your son's birth certificate?"

"I saw a school friend of Julian's wearing an eye patch. The girl's mother said they had seen Dr. Bella, but the eye kept getting worse."

Mrs. Sepulveda scribbled this down on a yellow legal pad.

"What were their full names?"

"I don't remember. She was an acquaintance, the mother of one of Julian's classmates. The mother was worried about finding enough money to pay for the prosthetic eye."

"Marisol, we need full names or we cannot make a case. What town was it, and what was the name of the clinic?"

"Zapopan. The I.N.I. Medical Post."

After Mrs. Sepulveda jotted this down, she arranged her notes and papers, then stood. "This is troubling news. I will do everything that I can to help. Thank you, all. Now, if you will please excuse me, I will make an appointment with the judge because I want your case to be heard as soon as possible."

"Will there be a trial?" Marisol asked.

"When the judge gets all of the information that I am going to get, he will make a judgment. I promise, that will be soon."

CHAPTER 29 DADDY

Carmen Bella got up out of the chair she had been slouching petulantly in, and began pacing around her father's home office in her sleek, white outfit. The room had bookshelves lining the wall near the door, and books rose to the ceilings. Part of the roomy office was a bar, complete with a mirror, and alabaster, female nudes. Dr. Bella looked like an accessory to her father's office.

Señor Castilano, a heavy set man with dignified, silver streaks in his trim hair and a frown accentuated by a drooping, thick mustache, held a letter from the judge in his hand. He cleared his throat and smoothed his mustache with his free hand, then began reading aloud, "It is recommended that Dr. Bella's two surviving accomplices will each serve one year in federal prison followed by one year of retraining to reform their characters and make them fit to work again. The crimes filed against them are kidnapping, assault and battery, cruelty to a patient, misuse of government property, and damage to said property." He raised his eyebrows and looked at her. She glared back at him.

He scowled and continued, "The hospital will pay a fine of four million pesos, to be distributed to said doctor's victims at a rate of 500,000 pesos each until all victims have been found. Any money remaining, if the victims or their families cannot be found, will be put in trust to pay for services for the blind. If the victims have died, the hospital will award the same amount to the victim's family, pending a review of the veracity of the case." He looked up and demanded of her, "How many were there?!!"

Her chin jutted in the air and she stared at him coldly, noticing his flabby jowls and wrinkles, the loose skin over his eyes. *The old hypocrite should get a little plastic surgery*, she thought. His drinking and smoking were beginning to show.

Her father shook his head when she didn't answer him. He continued, "As the nature of Dr. Bella's after hours appointments was not known by hospital administration, no criminal charges will be made; however, such visits and cash payments are clearly in opposition to the goal of protecting each patient and assuring consistent, quality care and public confidence in such care. It is the duty of the hospital's chief consultant to be aware of all transactions and medical provisions on the hospital's property. Therefore, the resignation of the hospital's chief consultant will be turned in to the ministry of health at the conclusion of this trial.

"The seriousness of Dr. Bella's crime is heightened in light of the fact that the aforementioned doctor is a federal specialist in ophthalmology. Dr. Carmen Bella is required to pay two million dollars. It is recommended that she serve not more than two years, and not less than eighteen months in a federal prison followed by three years extensive retraining. Following retraining, Dr. Bella will be on probation and closely monitored for one year and will have limited surgical duties. It is felt that Carmen Bella can be reformed, and her skills, which were learned in a government institution at expense to the state, should not be wasted."

At last the seriousness of the consequences pierced the convoluted and abnormal brain that lived in her hard little head. Her thin hard lips hung open and slack.

He leaned forward, and shouted at her, "You are a disgrace!"

Her body twitched in an instinctive startled reflex action like one who is whipped, but will not cry out. His eyes, trained as they were to watch for guilt and remorse, registered her reaction with a narrowing of his eyes, a pause and a satisfied nod.

He summed up the final details in his own words, "You are to begin serving your prison term in two weeks. They assume you won't jump bail, since the amount you posted is enough to wipe out your home, your mother's new home, and your pharmacy businesses." He pushed back his chair violently as he stood up, then he marched over and grabbed her by the shoulders. He growled, "Your credentials aren't worth spit now."

She had no answer for a few moments. Judging from the veins and the cord-like tendons standing out in his muscular neck, he looked like he might throttle her for ignoring him. She stifled a smile over her sick and minor triumph. At least she still had the power to upset him, which meant he cared a little. She jerked her arms away from his grasp and stepped back.

He bellowed at his daughter, "I got you an education and position. Eye specialist for the entire Guadalajara area! What made you do those things to those kids? When the ministry of health called me, was it almost two years ago already? I assured them that you were good to the country's peasants."

She looked away and redid her long, black ponytail while she gathered her thoughts. She had plenty of experience at meeting confrontation with a coolness that made her opposition appear foolish. She turned to him and calmly said, "Every one of those children had enough damage from their own accidents that they wouldn't have lived a fully-sighted life no matter what anyone did. Their infections alone would have robbed them of more than their sight. They would have been disfigured if not for me. Their parents couldn't afford any better, either.

"Besides, the children have family to help them when they have troubles. Me, I always got the minimum your sense of duty would allow. You couldn't marry me off, so you gave me an education to prevent me from disgracing you."

Her father began coughing. When he could breathe again, he said, "I couldn't let you become a little tramp like your mother. I knew I'd get no gratitude from you. You always were a spoiled ingrate! You never knew your place. You should have been giving me grandchildren, like your sisters did, not pecking out children's eyes like a scavenging old crow!" He cursed and ran his hands through his hair.

His face was becoming such a deep shade of red that, for an instant, Dr. Bella thought her father was going to cry, or worse, have a stroke. After a few moments, he walked back to his desk, fumbled around in his drawer, found and lit a cigarette. He took a deep drag, and then blew a long slow stream of smoke up at the light. He pulled up his chair and sat down heavily. He watched the smoke for a while, then stared at her briefly, and finally gazed at his bookshelves that were filled with law books.

The silence became unbearable for Carmen, and cruel words rolled easily off her tongue. "Why would I have children, just so some man could leave me with them to raise alone with no money, like you did to Ma?"

"What? Do you despise all men now?" His voice was now weak sounding. In fact, he spoke like a confused old man. "Is it my fault, that I lived with your mother for so long, although my parents forbade me?" He scratched his head, as if to this day, he didn't understand how he could have been in such a situation.

He said, "I thought she understood, but she tried to trap me with all those children. She couldn't even give me a boy. Still, you were my favorite once, because you were an intelligent girl. So, I gave you more than my other daughters."

247

Carmen Bella punctuated her sentences with definite articulations of her clever, small hands, when she said, "Yes, that's true since you gave them nothing! Except for paying my cheap tuition at a government-run university, a fee that's less than what you spend on your family for a couple of nice dinners, you haven't had a thing to do with us! The sons you have now with your young wife get whatever they want: property, houses, cars, positions that pay well – without all the hard work of schooling.

You could have at least helped me get a position in a private hospital that paid well. Our doctors sell pirated videotapes and CD's on the streets, that's how little money we make. The ear specialist sells "Gap" jeans in a booth downtown in order to afford a decent house in a safe area."

He smashed out his cigarette in a carved stone tray, leaned back in his chair, and looked at her wearily, one finger pushing on his eyebrow. He calculated his daughter's damage, took stock, as if deciding whether to sell. "I pleaded with you," he began calmly. "I said there is more to being a doctor than getting money, so stop being poisoned by the ideas of the United States. You gave gringos our children's eyes, for God's sake! You should go to prison, I swear, but I can't have any child of mine going there. Not now."

Carmen folded her arms in front of her and glared at her father. Her father's words worked upon her mind, transforming the large, silver bangle bracelets, which pressed against her breasts into an unwelcome vision of handcuffs. She unfolded her arms suddenly. "What are you going to do?"

"Maybe the judge will let you avoid prison by reforming your ways outside of the doctor's profession." He laughed. "You could sort mail without hurting anybody couldn't you? *Sí,* you could take bribes on the side, since that's what you love, for, say, fudging the postmark date." Then he sighed. "*Hija,* you are a great disappointment to me. You're as cruel as your mother." He got up and poured himself a tequila at the mirrored bar behind him.

Carmen watched his aging, but still handsome face. There had never been any man as intelligent, witty, or powerful as he. Even now as he disciplined her, she wanted his love, with an ache that she continuously pushed down. Once she began her practice, she'd thought that he would begin to extend invitations to his home, introduce her to the powerful people he knew, accept her again, the way he had before he abandoned her mother. But she discovered that she was still alone. This was an anomaly in Mexico, a person with no close family in a land of harsh economic realities, where extended family and its warmth was the survival of its people. People lived this way, the same as they combined beans and corn for protein in a semitropical desert, incapable of supporting many cattle, instead of eating beef daily like Americans. Now despite all of her money, she was still hungry and thirsty for love, but there would be none.

Her father sat down with his tequila and lime, and began sipping it thoughtfully. He got out an address book, and pulled his phone closer. *"Hija,* fetch me *The Comparative Labor Law Journal, The Federal Public Administration Manuel* and *Federal Civil Servant Labor Law.* The manuals are in the first set of shelves, near the middle, but the Journals are farther down."

She hurried, believing he could solve her legal problems. When she returned with the books, he was already pouring himself a second drink. He sipped slowly as he double-checked a few facts. Soon, he poised one hand over the phone, and finished his drink with the other, leaning back to get the last; he sucked between the ice cubes. Then he re-checked a phone number and dialed.

She remembered how much he drank each day. She still longed for the days when they had been close. He had enjoyed her spicy menudo soup, and he gave her a grand birthday party with a Piñata and hat dancers doing the cockroach dance when she was about eleven. She had been his favorite.

He stopped loving her mother around that time and her too, soon after that. He would corner mama and Carmen's older sisters and yell at them for hours. Once, Daddy drove the family out to a hot field of dry grass and thorns and made them all stand there, her included, while he berated them. Carmen hadn't understood the reason then, but it may have been someone's wastefulness, that was a word she'd heard shouted often. He also said he was ashamed of them. Their low class ways kept him from succeeding in his legal career. He drank a cold orange soda while they stood, hot, sticky, frightened, and trying to find the words that would appease him. She remembered clearly the dripping of the soda from the sides of his mouth, the gulping sounds he made, his Adam's apple moving, as she stood there panting and crying. That was before he left her mother with three daughters to raise alone and no money. Mama became cruel, and said often that money was all that mattered.

Since then, her Daddy had had other children, sons, with a new, socialite wife. Now, his position as District Attorney demanded that he keep appearances clean, and his former family, including her, out of the public eyes, and ears.

She had to accept whatever he decided before the drink altered his thinking and he lost his temper. Working at the post office wouldn't be so bad, not compared to the nasty jail she had spent a few weeks in recently. She watched her father make more phone calls. He was calling lawyers he knew.

As she halfway listened, she remembered Emilio, her medical assistant and sometime lover. He wouldn't get any special deals, and would have a tough time in prison, at first. But he was smart. He would work the situation to his advantage. His friend Raúl, the orderly who could lift larger patients with ease, would do well in prison, she mused. He was both homosexual and tough. Afonzo's effeminate homosexuality would have been in great demand had he lived. It was a pity he died.

Her father was saying into the phone, "Guanajuato is good enough. Yes, I appreciate that upper level positions are full right now; it doesn't matter. She will prove herself. You won't regret it. By the way, Oscar said you were interested in the Robles property on Lake Chapala, but there was a prior claim that came up while it was in escrow. Would you like me to see what I can do about that? I'd be glad to. I'll look into it first thing tomorrow!"

That stirred up her own property concerns. Her houses, the pharmaceutical businesses, could she keep those? She made her father a third drink, took out and lit a cigarette for him, and one for herself. Still on the phone, he slipped on his reading glasses and opened his law books as he listened to his friend's property troubles.

Señor Castilano accepted the drink, nodded to her, and waved her off. This was her signal to leave.

As she backed out the door, he was saying into the phone, "Ah, *sí*. That is true. Don't worry. They just need a little clarification on that matter. Sometimes even the best judges need a little guidance."

CHAPTER 30 RESTORATION

Near Dr. Bella's old clinic where Julian had found the needles, Julian and Ricky waited for the transfer bus to go to their private school for classes. A new, painted cloth sign on the front of the clinic said, "Now staffed by fully trained interns! Good care for reduced prices."

The bus pulled up to the private school. It was a modern structure, looking a bit like Enrique's blocks, partially knocked over and kicked. It had a fountain in front of the office, a block with water dribbling down its face. Julian and Ricky parted ways there. Ricky had advanced classes. Julian, however, took the regular ones because he had taken too much time off of school to chase after Dr. Bella, which he did not regret. Before that, he had goofed around because he was depressed, which he did regret.

The grounds were crowded, as usual, with students locking their bikes into the bike racks, leaning against the walls and chatting, some even sitting on the walls, which surrounded the school, dangling their feet and laughing. In the shaded halls, students opened and closed lockers noisily. A hurried glance at Julian's sport watch told him that class was about to begin, so he made his way to the class and took his seat at the front of the huge classroom.

There were soon seventy-five students filling all of the desks in his morning English class. The triple rows of windows were open, as usual. The teacher's podium was piled with notes, the blackboard had the date and the lesson plans on them, as well as this evening's homework. At a large, steel desk in the front corner, the teacher was finishing something, but looked up worriedly at Julian. Julian took out his planner and copied the homework down. The teacher glanced again at Julian, and carrying a sheaf of papers walked over to him, and spoke quietly.

"You got the homework? Good. Would you come out to the hall with me?"

Julian felt awkward. *What could it be?*

In the hallway, the teacher handed him the sheaf of papers. "These are the grammar worksheets for today. The police department has sent an officer to talk to you about something. If you're in any trouble, you know you can come talk to me. You've been a good student. Go to the office now, please."

The halls suddenly seemed so long, so quiet and so ominous. He envied the students who sat in their classes, untroubled, bored even. Even that would be better. Could someone have figured out that it was he who had hidden the seniors' PE uniforms in the science office? Maybe someone had seen him break into the computer lab. But it was only to get a cord for a teacher to borrow.

He looked over at the walls, longing to jump over them and head for the hills, the beach, anywhere. He resolved to face it, turned toward the office door, assumed the typical teenage hunchback look, and entered.

The secretaries were sitting in a huddle, even the normally garrulous secretary was quiet, eyes darting back and forth, peering through her heavy mask of makeup. Then, with a start, he felt, then saw, the heavy set, tall officer who was standing to his left. He looked about fifty and had a lot more stripes, ribbons, and badges on him than most officers. He vaguely remembered being introduced to this officer by the Guadalajara police and interviewed at the Puerto Vallarta hospital by him. He had been too upset to catch the name, or much else for that matter. He couldn't even remember what he'd told him. He again burned with shame briefly over what had almost happened to him.

"Julian?"

"Yeah."

"Remember me? Chief García. You've grown a bit, haven't you?" He reached out and patted Julian roughly on the shoulder with a bear-like paw.

Julian was tongue-tied. He nodded and stared at the chief, a habit that made him seem aloof, but he was, in fact, desperately frightened.

"I just want you to come with me for the afternoon to wrap up some unfinished business." Chief García waved to the still huddled secretaries and guided Julian out the door by means of a firm hand to the boy's broad, but thin shoulder.

Once in the police car, Julian examined the marvelous dashboard: the two-way radio, the rifle, the laptop and other things he couldn't recognize. The car dipped when the Chief lowered his bulk into it. "You like all those technological wiz bangs, don't you?" he said.

Julian smiled a little, "Yeah. I could enjoy working with that stuff. Except for getting shot at, and seeing creeps go free after you catch them, it would be all right being a policeman, I guess."

Chief García's bushy eyebrows practically disappeared under his peppery forelock. "So, other than those drawbacks, you have an interest in chasing criminals, ay? Well how about that? Yes, you have experienced it and come out all right."

"Thanks." Julian smiled. Maybe this was cool after all.

"There is, however, one little matter that must be cleared up by you, son. A good cop never steals – and no young man should either."

Julian's ears started burning. His knees, chin, and even his elbows began trembling. The gun. Now he must pay for having stolen it. He had dreaded and even expected this moment for a while. Had nightmares about it, for a month, but at last he'd believed it would not be addressed. He began to sweat. *What now. Oh, what now?* he thought. The officer reached back and lifted a metal, gray box from the back seat, deftly unlocked it, and lifted the lid. Chief García paused to watch all of Julian's expressions and judge, from his vast experience with teen boys in trouble, whether or not this boy was ready to redeem himself.

Julian stared at the gun. He remembered the lies he had told Señora Neri, and the bruises on her face. Then the memory of Raúl, who had tried to enter him, crashed into his consciousness with violence. He imagined the warm metal of the gun, heavy in his hand as he'd fumbled for it that night. It had been worth anything to avoid that! It had been worth anything to slow down Dr. Bella's murdering orderlies. He instinctively gripped his arm where the searing bullet had torn into his arm, in retaliation for using that gun.

"Brings back some bad memories, doesn't it? There is something you must do. It will help you feel better about some of those memories."

Julian was still fearful, but curious. He shrank back into the bucket seat.

"You must return the gun to Señor Neri."

"By myself? He will –"

Chief García closed and locked the box with the gun inside. "No, not by yourself. I am going with you. In fact, Señor Neri is expecting us."

Julian's legs began to shake. His eyes were wide. "Now? You mean we're going to go now? I don't think I'm ready. I don't know what to say."

"Don't worry. You've got time to think while we drive there. Buckle up." Chief García turned the ignition, threw his big arm across the back of Julian's seat, and craned his head to look behind them for traffic. As soon as the street was clear, the police car took off with all of the authority it should have. The engine purred. Julian tried to focus on the sound, and watch the technology in the car, yet he squirmed in his seat, looking back at his school as a place of haven, and wished he were back in class. What could he say to Señor Neri? The man had trusted him with a good paying job, rare to be had by anyone, much less a boy. His wife had trusted him with her important papers in her desperate moments during Señor Neri's kidnapping. The enormity of his breach of faith with people close to him now struck him. Never good with words, Julian was about to be faced with bridging a gap like a canyon with words as flimsy as grass ropes; it seemed impossible. The worst part was that he alone had created that loss of trust with people who were like family.

After a long silence, they passed an ugly street, lined with gaudy billboards where the airport was, and Julian realized that soon they would be going through the heart of the city, and close to the Neri's home. Beginning to panic, he said, "Chief, I don't know what to say to them!"

"Well, son, how do you feel about what you did?"

"I'm mixed up about it. I am sorry that I lied to Señora Neri. She was nice to me. And, I'm sorry because now Señor Neri can't trust me to work for him anymore – or at least, I wouldn't. But, if I hadn't had that gun with me –" He broke off, unable to explain.

"What would have happened?"

"Something too horrible to talk about, and I won't!"

As usual, traffic was crazy. Even around a police car, the traffic careened close by, almost hitting side mirrors, although there were fewer pedestrians darting out in front. The chief was very busy negotiating the traffic, but after a pause, and a soft muttering under the breath, he replied. "Just tell the truth, as much as you can. Explain how you feel about it, like you just did to me. It is best for you. It is for you that I do this, so you will grow up to be a fine man like your father was."

"I didn't know that you knew him."

"We were acquainted. It was tragic what happened to him, a good man like that. Died of a broken heart for your beautiful little sister. You have suffered many losses, Julian. Unfortunately, I know a lot of boys who need a second chance. And you deserve it more than any other boy I know. But a new start won't happen for you until you make amends. I had to learn that myself one time. I used to drink too much and I had a big mouth. My life has been much better since I realized that and tried to do something about it."

No grown-up had ever confessed anything like that to him. Julian stared for a moment at the chief's profile.

Soon Julian and chief García stood at the great door. The sweat from being in the hot police car was evaporating, but a different kind of perspiration was collecting in his sparse mustache now.

Before the chief knocked, he slipped the gray box containing the gun into Julian's hand, saying, "You are not fully a man until you seek the forgiveness of another man. Now is your chance." The chief rapped on the door with an iron doorknocker.

Instead of the customary callings and announcements at the door, the two visitors were hustled by a young maid through the glass sliding doors and into the cool, almost forest-like backyard. Julian noticed that the trees he had planted were grown almost two feet taller since almost a year and a half ago when he had planted them.

Señor Neri came out soon after, wearing a cream colored, traditional shirt, the kind that was pleated in the front and designed to be cool. He shook his guests' hands warmly.

Julian wondered if he would be so warm toward him after he heard what Julian had to say. Or had the chief already told him what this was about? It was odd to see Señor Neri so friendly and outgoing. Julian hadn't even seen Señor Neri like that on his boat or when he had been drinking.

Señora Neri, however, smiled tightly, not warmly, the way she used to before the gun turned up missing.

Julian shrugged, ashamed, when she had asked him what he would like to drink. Señor Neri took this as his cue to take over, a move which was customary for him, and he ordered for everyone, "Lemonade for Julian, and the chief – who is of course, on duty – and a bourbon and water for me."

They seated themselves at a large, white, wicker patio set in Señor Neri's spacious backyard. Julian remembered the day he had overheard Señor Neri dismiss his bodyguards. He looked around and didn't see anyone that looked like replacements. Perhaps being friends with the chief of police was enough.

The chief said, "Señora Neri, Julian has something he wants to tell you."

At that moment, Julian realized he really did want to apologize to Señora Neri. He swallowed and nodded his head vigorously.

Under the table, Julian was gripping the heavy, gray box with both hands. His reason for being there had not left his mind for a second. He tried to speak. He lost focus on the men around him. His mind seemed to spin, and the conversation only came to him in colorful fragments, like a child's kaleidoscope.

Señor Neri was saying, "I wouldn't mind taking a boat trip tomorrow. You two want to come?"

The chief smiled slyly, and licked the lemonade from his mustache, so thick like the rest of him. "You know Saturdays are my busiest days, but I'll bet the muchacho here could make it. Right, Julian?"

"I.... That was the best day, when we went boating with Victor. I'll always remember," he babbled, feeling stupid. "I don't know how you could invite me now, though – after what I did to you – to both of you." He put the gray box on the table and pushed it toward Señor Neri. "I shouldn't have stolen your gun. You helped me. Both of you did." He glanced at Señora Neri.

Señora Neri had one eyebrow raised comically. Her lips were pursed. Julian swallowed. "I lied to you, Señora. I am sorry that I did that. I stole the gun and lied about it because I hated Dr. Bella so much. I wasn't thinking clearly." He bit his lip and waited.

Señor Neri opened the gray box and took out the gun. He slid open the top with a loud click and checked to see if it was loaded. It wasn't. He put it back and closed the lid. It seemed like Señor Neri, at least, was ready to let it go. He looked to Señora Neri.

She sighed and half-smiled at Julian. "Yes. I will forget it now."

"Except for one thing, Julian," Señor Neri said, "You're gonna work off what you did. One month working on the boat and on the garden with no pay. After that, you can resume your old job, if you like."

Julian nodded, and said, "Yeah, okay." Then he shuddered and asked worriedly, "But you don't need any more trees planted, do you?"

Señor Neri laughed and clapped him on the back, "No, but I have these bushes...." And he swung his arm behind him to indicate about twenty shrubs lined up like soldiers ready for battle, each wearing a big green, bucket for a boot.

The chief and Señora Neri laughed.

Julian's jaw dropped and his hand went to his cheek. He turned to them and smiled. He said, "Señor Neri, the sooner your yard is completely filled with plants and no dirt left to put anything into, the better!"

Chief García said, "Your father would be proud of you, son. And your mother seems to like Victor. She's too good for that scoundrel, but he really cares for her. She deserves to be happy. Don't ever forget that. Well, I'd best take you home now, Julian." He rose, and the others did too.

CHAPTER 31 PRINT IT

At 3am, the huge, gray presses clacked and whirred, and the smell of ink and solvent filled the warm air of the news floor. The news was good on Tuesday, July 3, 2001. Victor's paper was filled, like many papers around the world, with stories about President Fox marrying his girlfriend on the previous morning, a year of democracy for Mexico.

Victor took a revised article from the lead pressman's ink-stained hands and read it. It stated that Dr. Carmen Bella had resigned, and would no longer be serving in the Puerto Vallarta clinic, nor in the Guadalajara hospital, nor in the neighboring villages. The reporter boldly stated the reasons for Dr. Bella's leaving, and asked about the numbers of patients. If any of her former patients needed further care – it said – or had any complaints about previously received eye care, they should contact Dr. Suarez. It stated that Dr. Suarez had proven himself very reliable in spite of his youth, and having completed his internship a year ago, now had enough practice to be the eye *especialista* for the area. The article listed several numbers to call for Dr. Suarez, depending on the type of treatment one needed. The article even had the story about Julian, recently updated with news from his mother. This was Victor's exclusive story.

"That will do it," he declared happily, handing the article back to the pressman who smiled and strode back to the editor waving the paper in the air and shouting, "*Sí, está bien.*" Victor was still as frightened of printing the truth today as he ever was, but now he gladly resolved to print the truth anyway.

He knew instinctively, vaguely, why Dr. Bella wasn't in prison. Yet, he hoped that through his reporting, he could help his people get to the bottom of it. He smiled when he saw, rather than hear over the noise, his editor cheering. He felt a deep friendship for this man who had filled in for him during his long absence.

Victor nervously went back to his desk and collapsed there. He leaned back in his chair, cradled his forehead in his hand and his overwrought mind began to spin.

If his best friend hadn't been kidnapped, or if his best friend's brother hadn't loved Julian, Victor would have been content publishing news as safe and bland as baby food.

Marisol was partly responsible for his new feelings toward his newspaper as well. She had criticized him harshly when they all departed Guadalajara.

Her hair had been tightly coiled, and her glaring eyes reflected the sun's brightness. She had looked like the furious snake goddess Coatilcue when she'd said, "Why don't you have the courage to print the whole truth about Dr. Bella in your paper? When Javier was kidnapped, and when the drug cartel leader died while getting plastic surgery, people found out the whole truth eventually, just not from you."

265

He had laughed and joked that with clever women like her spreading the news, maybe *he* didn't need to.

It occurred to him that it would be lonely at home, where he should now be going to get some sleep. Then, he nodded off in his chair. He was soon awakened by his editor.

"*¡Es una buena día, Jefe!*" The editor called out, smiling under his round, professorial glasses.

The pressmen were smiling, too, many with missing, or tobacco stained teeth. There was an air of celebration and much joking about the effects their prized story would have on the bourgeois.

The warm, solvent and ink scented air floated toward him. He felt rejuvenated as he watched his younger workers stacking and loading papers into the backs of the trucks.

The few educated readers who had the money and time to sip strong coffee while they read the news would pass on the information, until eventually everyone would know what had been happening to Dr. Bella's young patients.

He definitely wanted some strong coffee. The large steel urn was empty. Everyone was running on adrenaline. He brewed enough coffee for his crew. Then he took a cup as soon as he could. He spilled some and obsessively wiped it clean, even though thirty feet away grease, dirt, and ink congealed on and around numerous large and noisily whirring, clanking machines.

As he sipped his coffee, he realized that he wanted to thank Marisol for telling him to print the truth, for raising a boy like Julian, and for something else. He wasn't quite sure what. Hell, he needed to talk to her, to see her.

He looked outside to see the sky turning a deep shade of blue. Dawn would come soon.

Streaks of pink shone above the jagged roofline of the offices and factories that stood behind his building. Today would be a fine day to romance a good woman. His mood thus brightened, he went back to work until 10am. He called Marisol. No answer. An hour later, he called again. Still no answer, and the paper had gone out hours ago. His editor came by and asked if he'd like to come eat lunch with his family. Victor smiled and declined. Soon the building was empty again, as it would be for a few hours. He called again.

"*Hola.*"

"Marisol, it's Victor. The story went out today, the whole thing. Can I bring you a copy and take you out to lunch?"

"Oh, that's nice, but I have to go back to work in a couple of hours. I was just making myself a quick lunch at home, since I don't have a house to clean right now."

"Could I come by at least, and bring the newspaper? You will like this article. *¿Por favor?*"

There was a pause. "Yes, I'd like that."

267

"Good. I'll be there in about twenty minutes, unless you'd like me to pick up some enchiladas. They are so good that I eat them every day for lunch."

She laughed. "The same thing every day? Just come over, I'll fix you something different."

When he hung up, he began humming a Maríachi tune absently, wearing a little, contented smile. He pulled his jangling keys out of the drawer, and didn't even stop to check the mirror in the small, dirty bathroom. He knew he needed another shave, and there was dirt under his nails, but he was in a hurry. He quickly strode out to the back of the press floor and snatched a paper from the stack of extras the business kept for the workers and for historical filing. He breathed deeply the wonderful inky smell on the fresh papers that filled the air as he folded the paper lovingly and tucked it under his arm.

CHAPTER 32 REWARD

In April 2001, Julian's mother received a notice to pick up a certified letter from the post office. Never having received such a notice before, she thought it meant she was in some kind of trouble, and fear gripped her heart. She immediately re-planned her route so that she could stop by between the four house cleanings, the shopping and meal preparations for two American and two Mexican homeowners. After cleaning the first home, she had to buy food for a catered meal she was to prepare, so a trip to the post office would fit well there in the late morning hours, she decided.

She waited briefly in line at the dimly lit post office. Her skin was still moist from the exertion of cleaning and walking through the warm, humid streets.

The sun barely pierced the dirty, post office's windows, plastered as they were with advertisements and notices. When it was her turn to step up to the barricade-like high counter, she unsnapped her large handbag and fished out the notice. Nervously, she handed it to the clerk. The clerk took a long time to return, but handed her the official looking envelope without comment. She was fearful of opening it in that office, so she walked half a block away first.

Inside the envelope was a check from the civil hospital, an award of 1,000,000 pesos, and a letter. She read the letter, which contained an apology and an explanation that each of the known victims was receiving a similar check. It said that she should feel comfortable with the services at the civil hospitals in Puerta Vallarta and Guadalajara and that these hospitals had excellent safety records.

"Hm!" She said aloud.

Marisol walked to a nearby cathedral, crossed herself before the virgin Guadalupe holding the infant Jesus, and knelt between two wooden pews. There in the cool, incense-filled haven, surrounded by the holy saints and celestial, colored windows, she began weeping.

She showed Julian the letter that evening in the fading light at the cluttered, but clean, kitchen table. Her eyes had dark circles beneath them.

He read it twice. "Why are you so upset, Mama? This is great news! Look, it says Dr. Bella resigned and gave up her doctor's credentials. She won't practice any kind of medicine ever again!" then he looked up at her, his eyes fixed on her face to watch for her every expression.

She smiled gently, then sighed and leaned back against the sink. "Yes, that's good, but why no prison time for that butcher? She just as bad as a drug runner or a gangster."

"At least she is out of business. It says she had pharmacy businesses too, but the government took them. Look at this check again, Mama." He held it up and waved it like a victory flag. "That's a lot of money!" He grinned.

Her arms crossed, but she nodded slightly in concession. "I wonder why she wasn't fired?"

"Mom, they fired her. They always say that this police chief resigned, or that cabinet member resigned when they get caught. Our history teacher told us they do it that way."

The front door opened and closed. Enrique bounded in and pulled on his mother's arms. "*Mami,* I'm hungry."

"*Uno momento, Pobrecito,*" she said, petting his hair absent-mindedly.

Julian got up from the chair at the table and put his hands under Enrique's arms and lifted him up for a crushing hug, causing Enrique to giggle. He took his little brother back to his lap when he sat down.

"What's the matter?" he asked, while bouncing Enrique on his leg a little.

"It's a good amount of money, Julian." She smiled a little at him. "It's just that I don't think she has been punished enough to pay back what she did to María and all those children I saw in the clinic. They were in our village. They played with you and ate papayas in our backyard. Losing a job not a harsh enough consequence for what she tried to do to you, and would have done if God hadn't sent our American friends."

271

Julian put Enrique back on his feet and got up. "I'm going to call them now, Mama."

Alan was making use of the sunny spring weather by building a new bathroom addition with his hired man when he got the call. He held a board up with one hand and pulled the phone off his belt with the other. When Julian finished telling him the contents of the letter and the amount of the check, Alan said, "Well, I'll be damned. Are you about ready for a vacation, Julian? Good, because you're going to come up and stay with us awhile. You're going to get your new lens now."

Julian, at seventeen years of age, was considered to be grown to his adult size, and the reparations money would help pay for the operation. That night, when Alan told Lena the news, they celebrated by enjoying a special dinner and calling several friends to tell them.

Lena scheduled a June appointment for Julian with the very much in demand Dr. Fishman to receive an acrylic lens in the United States. This was an involved process because the schedules for the anesthesiologist, and the retina specialist all had to match up.

Lena also made arrangements for Ricky to fly to the United States with Julian. The boys would stay at Alan and Lena's house for a month. This gave her time with their grandson, and would help their daughter, Audrey, and son-in-law, Manuel, have more time to run their lumber business and resort.

When Alan told Dr. Fishman Julian's story, the doctor said that he would do the operation for free. In fact, the doctor called Alan later to say that all of the specialists and the hospital itself would donate their services. When Alan told Lena that the hospitals were donating their services, she demanded to know exactly how the conversation went.

"I just told them the story," Alan said, "and they wanted to help."

Alan told the story again, with the added detail that he had told the story to the airlines, and they decided to give Julian a half-price ticket.

Lena said, "I can't believe you!" shaking her head, but grinning.

Since this left a large sum of money, the money could be saved for Julian's college expenses and to raise his mother and brother's standard of living.

On the day of the operation, in June, Julian was so worried that he woke up in a sweat and remembered snatches of grim nightmares. In fact, he had been worried for many weeks, but he had joked about it calmly. In the morning, he and Ricky were in the Todd's recreation room, amidst the many antiques and oil paintings that weren't quite good enough to display in their main house. Before the boys got out of their sleeping bags, they lay talking. Julian and Ricky were enjoying the fact that they didn't have to get up early for school, and that their mothers were far away for a time. The boys couldn't have been more excited if they woke up on Mars, or at least, in Disneyland.

They planned their fishing trip a little and talked about basketball. Julian was growing more excited. Then they talked about how at home, their mothers would wake them up and put them to work. Julian mimicked each of their mothers in a falsetto voice, "Ricky, get up and help your dad load those twenty boxes of fragile plates and cups on the motorboat." He pointed at Ricky and then towards some imaginary boat.

Next he put one arm around an imaginary small boy that apparently had been stashed in his sleeping bag with him. He shook his other finger at Ricky. He spoke, exaggerating every syllable and rolling his eyes. "Julian, take your brother *everywhere* you go and watch him because I've got four houses to clean today."

Julian lay back down and frowned at a painting of a young, nude girl bathing. The boys had unanimously decided on their first night, with much laughter, that this painting was the best in their room and Alan certainly had good taste.

Ricky propped himself up on one elbow and asked Julian, "Are you nervous about going to the doctor today?"

Julian said, "No. The doctors here are good, they say. It's like they do miracles."

Then he looked at Ricky and smiled. "Worse, if they make my eye too healthy, I might go into shock when I can clearly see you. You look funny enough now!" He held up his arms, karate style for protection from the retribution he knew would soon follow.

Ricky whooped and pelted him with pillows.

Later that day, Julian felt helpless and anxious in the blue surgery cap and gown at first, but a very nice nurse had given him medication to make him drowsy and mellow. Doctor Fishman came in and told him to keep his eyes open, and this wouldn't hurt, but it would take all of his concentration to hold still and look at the poster above him. He stared up at the poster of the Swiss Alps for 30 minutes while the nurses shined multiple lights in his eyes. He never saw or felt the lens that was inserted, shot-like, as his eye was numb, and the doctor entered the side of Julian's eyeball, careful to keep it out of Julian's line of sight. The doctor had explained the procedure to Alan, who had explained it to Julian before his surgery. The lens was a small acrylic square-like shape that would expand and hold once it was inside his eye.

Afterwards the surgery, everything looked blurry, but the nurse explained that when the drops they had given him to dilate his eyes wore off, "You'll be able to see the answers on the papers of kids who sit across the room from you, when you get back to school!"

He was a little wobbly when he got into Alan and Lena's van, and he promptly fell asleep during the drive home.

At home, Lena woke him. "Julian, wake up." Then said, "Alan, help him to his room."

Alan was shorter than Julian, but wider and stronger, and they made slow, steady progress up the curved staircase. Julian hazily wondered why people wanted so many stairs in their houses. As Alan tucked him into the guest bed, Julian marveled that Alan and Lena were so nice to him, but he missed his mother.

When he woke up from his nap and came down to the living room, he found Alan, Lena and Ricky gathered around the coffee table, playing Poker and making ten cent bets as they frequently did in the evenings. Lena was the first to ask, "How do you feel? Let me see you." She got up and took his face in her hands.

"My eye hurts, like there is some sand in it," he said, feeling confused.

Now Alan looked at Julian's eye. "Look up. Good. Now look to the left. Right. Down." He patted Julian on the back and indicated with a gesture that he should sit down. "Um, I think he's going to be all right. Let's let him sleep tonight, and I will call the doctor in the morning. Christ, he just had surgery. A little blood in the eye isn't a disaster. It used to happen to my friends and I when we went diving sometimes." He rubbed his hands together and leaned toward the boys, "We'd go really deep you see. We had tons of equipment and abalone. When it was time to return to the surface…"

So Alan told the boys another one of his stories and soon they were all playing cards again. Julian beat Alan, and gleefully scooped up a pile of dimes.

CHAPTER 33 20 - 20

Almost two weeks after the operation, Julian went to the upstairs bathroom following a game of pool with Ricky, which he had lost even though he could see perfectly. He washed his hands, smoothed his hair down and checked to see if he still looked the same. His eye now looked clear and normal. He was good-looking, with the almond-eye shape of the Aztecs, but with the Spanish high cheekbones and nose. His wavy hair had grown long again, like St. Joseph's. Satisfied by his reflection today, he bounded down the stairs easily; for each stair was clearly behind the other in succeeding order, and each foot landed surely where he put it. Julian laughed, and then pulled the huge front door open and leapt through it.

Alan was turning a wrench on an intake pipe to Lena's new fountain in the front yard. When Julian appeared, Alan stopped and wiped the sweat from his eyes. He stared as Julian danced down the porch. He smiled and shouted, "What the devil has gotten into you?"

Julian bounded past, saying, "Hi there, Grandpa!"

Alan sat back on his heels and chuckled. Lena came from the pool and stood at the gate beside the house, wrapping a robe around her. Ricky followed in his dripping swim trunks.

"What's going on?" Lena asked.

"Julian must be excited that he can see clearly again." Alan said, cheerfully squinting up at Julian, who was at that moment running through the apple orchard.

Suddenly, Julian cried out in pain. Alan saw that Julian had just discovered the deer fence and laughed, "Now that you can see, watch where you're going!"

Lena and Ricky laughed. Julian scowled at all of them, feeling embarrassed and rubbing his leg as he walked back down the slope.

Ricky began to drag Julian to the pool, laughing and teasing. Alan laughed too, and put his arm affectionately around Lena. Ricky was ready to toss a willing Julian in when Lena said, "Stop them, Alan!"

Alan put his hand to his lips, whistled loudly, and they froze. He said, "He's not ready for that yet. Be a little careful for awhile."

Julian said, "Aww…I'm fine," and then slumped down on a deck chair that was shaded by a large umbrella.

Ricky leaned close to Julian and looked innocently at him with his big green eyes. He asked, "When we get back to Vallarta, are you going to put your eyes to some good use and help our baseball team start winning again?"

Julian weighed this idea for a tenth of a second and nodded, "I'll be there."

Ricky smiled, his white teeth sparkling, and said, "I know where else you'll be. You'll be getting caught up with the cute girls you've been missing, right?" and punched Julian in the shoulder lightly.

Lena laughed and said, "I hope he gets caught up at school first."

"I will," Julian said, "Besides, I don't need to get caught up with *all* the girls - just with one."

CHAPTER 34
ESTHER'S WEDDİNG

The altar of the Our Lady of Guadalupe Church was aglow with candles. To the left of the altar, María sat at the piano, playing a melodic love song. The large Puerta Vallarta church was packed with excited friends and family, children, and babies. The aisles were almost blocked with extra folding chairs draped in flowing, white fabric.

"Doesn't María play beautifully?" Manuel asked, nuzzling Audrey's shoulder with his chin.

Audrey softened, and snuggled up to him. Then she turned around with the crowd and watched Esther's little sister, the flower girl, at the door looking adorable in a burgundy satin dress. Next, her four-year old brother came up the aisle carrying the rings. For a few moments, he stopped and looked questioningly at his mother. He ambled into the pews briefly towards her, and the packed church rippled with polite laughter. His mother waved him on frantically. He finally proceeded up to the altar, to everyone's amused smiles and exchanged looks.

Finally, Esther and her stout father arrived at the door to the church. Esther smiled radiantly and graciously. When Esther walked up the aisle beside her happy looking father, wearing a black suit and tie, Audrey felt relieved. The father was beaming at his daughter now.

Esther's advanced pregnancy was nicely concealed by the lace dress María and her mother, Rosa, had made. She looked like a queen. The lace veil that María had made by hand cascaded behind Esther's face and down her back. Meanwhile, her groom waited at the altar, looking scholarly with his glasses and thin build. He removed his glasses to wipe his eyes with a furtive motion. The depth of his feeling for Esther was clear, in spite of how delayed the wedding had been.

The sermon went on for about an hour, punctuated by candle lightings, songs, musical solos, and good wishes from various relatives. There were also many hearty responses from the congregation. It was moving for almost everyone, judging from the crying and the tears of joy Audrey saw and heard all around her. Among those who were not moved by the service, were the babies who had to be frequently rushed out, and the little children who could not quite be hushed.

When the priest concluded his sermon, the bride and groom exchanged rings. Then the priest wrapped a ribbon around the newlyweds to signify that they were now a family unit, sacred to the community. Esther and her new husband faced the community in the pews.

Audrey noticed the slick hair of Victor's head next to Marisol's simple, but elegantly coifed hair. *At least those two had found each other somehow through all of this trouble*, she thought.

The newlyweds slowly glided down the aisle, smiling at each recognized face.

After other guests had departed for the reception, Audrey and her husband stayed behind to gather the decorations. The afternoon sun was slanting into the now emptying church. She wiped a tear from the corner of her eye and surveyed the ribbons and flowers, which needed taking down.

She was startled when Manuel grasped her arm.

He asked, "Can I help you?"

She scanned his face, hoping he hadn't seen her cry. She gave him a quick kiss. "Sure. Make sure all this stuff goes into Esther's brother's car and they know to bring it into the reception hall."

Manuel helped her to remove the candles and swags of flowers from the walls and candelabras. Next, she sent him to clean out the groomsmen's changing room while she gathered Esther's things from the bridesmaids' rooms. She fumed, *He was so damn helpful to her, but such a know-it-all, too. He and Julian could have been killed!* She threw the flowers and Esther's stuff in the trunk and slammed it. Nearby, Manuel winced slightly.

Everyone had already gathered at the reception hall by the time she and Manuel arrived. They were seated by a walker at a table with Ricky, Julian, María, Marisol, and Victor.

As the guests were served wine, Audrey complimented María and her mother on the fantastic lacework in Esther's veil and shawl and in the decorations and table coverings now were surrounding them.

María said, "Thank you. Lace work doesn't bother me now the way it used to. It used to irritate my eyes."

After a moment of stunned silence, Julian began to laugh loudly and the rest of those at the table began to laugh, nervously at first, then letting loose when they saw that María was laughing too. Those at the nearby tables heard their laughter and raised their glasses to them.

When the laughter died down, María continued her explanation why she enjoyed making lace. "I can listen to my new radio or even my new television if the novelas are on, and I just feel the thread to know it is going the way it should go to become something beautiful and useful."

Julian whispered something to María.

María resembled a person enjoying music with her eyes closed. Audrey smiled at Manuel, who smiled back at her. Then he breathed a sigh of relief.

At the other end of the room, Esther's oldest brother, Raphael, wearing a Maríachi-style embroidered hat and pants with the silver studs down the sides, gave a short speech on behalf of Esther and her new husband.

The entire ceiling of the hall fluttered with bright, multicolored, hand-cut tissue papers, as if clapping along with the crowd's swelling applause. Soon the guests were served rich, chicken mole and lobsters, followed by custards.

Afterwards, it was time to dance to the music of Raphael's Maríachi band. Except for a few ancient grandparents, everyone danced: some danced with a baby in their arms for a turn, mothers danced with children, girls danced with each other, and the men chose freely from among the available ladies, including their spouses, female relatives, or the children.

Julian and María got up to dance together. Audrey watched Julian's arms folded around María, her long hair woven between his strong, young arms. María and Julian's ordeal suddenly seemed bittersweet to her, like gritty, spiced, Mexican chocolate.

Marisol, who was sitting next to Victor, and Audrey exchanged smiles and then they both watched Julian and María dancing. The young couple swayed back and forth together, the way people do who do not really know how to dance. Julian flashed a grin at his mother and Audrey over María's shoulder, and then he closed his eyes and hugged María tightly.

A SPECIAL NOTE FROM
DOCTOR FISHMAN:

"It was easy to arrange for the donation of the hospital and anesthesia services. They were very happy to help. The hospital was Los Gatos Community Hospital.

The eye had been previously injured with a sharp object and we put in a plastic implant (interocular lens). The implant was also donated by the manufacturer.

I remember that your parents were very dedicated to helping the child, and that they arranged all of his care and transportation."

-Martin L. Fishman, MD, MPA

ABOUT THE
AUTHOR:

Tara Moore graduated from San Jose State University, with a BA, in 1984, a Multiple Subject Teaching Credential in 1996, a Single Subject Teaching Credential in 2005, and a MA in English in 2007. She has two children, has served eight years in the U.S. Navy Reserves, and has been teaching English for almost twenty years in San Jose, California.